Bottle of Uncertainty

Bottle of Uncertainty. Copyright 2019 by Katie Melko. All rights reserved. Printed in the United States of America. For information, 12 Paws Publishing, LLC.

The Library of Congress has catalogues the paperback edition as follows:

ISBN Information 978-1-5323-9287-0

Bottle of Uncertainty

Katie Melko

12 Paws Publishing, LLC

This book is dedicated to my husband, James. I love you so much and couldn't have done this without your love and support.

And to my mom, who always inspires me to go for my dreams and is always standing by my side. I love you <3

To my family and my tribe: Thank you for always being there for me.

Acknowledgements:

Thanks go out to my editor and all the people who worked on this

project.

We do not believe in ourselves until someone reveals that deep inside

us something is valuable, worth listening to, worthy of our trust,

sacred to our touch. Once we believe in ourselves, we can risk

curiosity, wonder, spontaneous delight or any experience that reveals

the human spirit.

-E.E. Cummings

Bottle of Uncertainty

Prologue

1977- Massachusetts

Fifteen-year-old Kathleen Ramsey was a student at Medford High School, she mainly kept to herself and her studies. She was by no means popular. Kathleen always had her eye on a Senior in school, but it was just a fantasy. Camila and her use to always dream about their crushes and giggle to each other.

One morning, Jeremy approached Kathleen as she was walked into school. He leaned against a pillar smoking a cigarette. Jeremy wore a leather jacket and motorcycle boots with his denim jeans and tee. "Hey there, Kat." as he nodded in her direction.

"Hi…" Kathleen looked confused and turned around to make sure he was actually speaking to her. Jeremy was 17 years old with black hair, green eyes, and pale skin.

Jeremy smiled at her as he ran his hand through his hair. "Want to go to my prom with me?" His green eyes pierced her brown eyes intently.

"Um… yes. I would, if you are serious." She stammered back, her cheeks flushed matching her strawberry-blonde hair, her freckles barely be seen.

Jeremy smirked, "Pick you up at 7 next Friday then." As he walked away, with his leather jacket flipped over one shoulder.

This was one of the things that Kathleen melted over, she found him to be very attractive and mysterious. She couldn't believe he was interested in her. Kathleen's geek exterior with her coke bottle glasses. She often wore Ked shoes and jeans with baggy tops to hide her imperfect body that she didn't like.

When Jeremy picked her up that following Friday, Kathleen half thought he wouldn't show. "Hi…" Kathleen stammered as she came down in her dress.

"Do you say anything else but hi" Jeremy joked. "You look beautiful!" As he put out his arm to take hers.

Blushing, "You look sexy… I mean handsome too." Mortified she looked down at the floor.

"I liked the first answer better. Ready to have some fun?" Jeremy asked with a smirk on his face.

Her parents took pictures and waved them off as they walked to the car. She constantly felt she had to remind herself to breathe. He was so sexy and intimidating to her. Her fantasy of Jeremy was a reality and she didn't know what to do with it. Prom was fun, he danced and gave her all the attention she could dream of and that night she lost her virginity to Jeremy. Kathleen thought that Jeremy was her soul-mate and floated home on cloud-9.

She was overwhelmed by the attention dating Jeremy got her. She would stutter or not say much at all in conversation. Kathleen was awkward and excelled at one thing, school. She was incredibly smart and a good hearted person, but in high school everything was about the exterior image and Kathleen's got her nothing but jokes and laughter. Jeremy put a stop to all of that. He loved how brilliant she was and how she would help him with his homework. He always gave her just the right attention to sway her into doing his work.

Little did Kathleen know how uncool and mean Jeremy was, but she was young and thought she was in love. She would sit outside under a willow tree in her parents' yard and dream about life with Jeremy. At the time, Kathleen thought he was her be-all end-all and they would live happily ever after. How untrue that was, for Kathleen had marked her fate to go in a completely different path. Jeremy was a senior and Kathleen was a sophomore. They would talk about college and their future often. Kathleen always wanted to be a nurse, while Jeremy strived to be a mechanic and would go to technical school after he graduated.

Kathleen was top of her class but had only one friend, Camila, and most of the time; they were picked on for their lack of style and old clothes. Camila was an only child and Kathleen had become like her sister. She was the only true friend Kathleen would ever have. Camila didn't like Jeremy and would tell Kathleen often to be careful. Jeremy and Camila didn't get along, and he would make fun of her constantly. This irritated Kathleen, but never could muster the courage to speak out about it. Jeremy didn't seem to care about any of that though, he was always more concerned with her helping him graduate and their physical relationship. That all changed when Kathleen lost her virginity and got pregnant all within the same month. She was fifteen and scared, she didn't know what to do or how to tell her parents.

Jeremy was livid, screaming at her, "This is not happening, get rid of it. It will ruin our life."

Kathleen was crying and mortified by his outbursts, "You told me you pulled out. You said we'd be fine. How did you let this happen?"

That was the first time Jeremy hit her. He slapped her across the face so hard she fell backwards, shocked and upset. She looked up at him with tears in her eyes, holding her cheek and Jeremy looked right at her pointing his finger at her. "Don't you ever talk to me like that again!" Jeremy stormed off leaving her sitting on the ground crying.

She called Camila who scooped her up and took her home, consoling her without judgment. Promising that it would be okay, she would be fine, and it was better this way to leave him behind. She didn't deserve his abuse. Kathleen and Camila went to her home and told her parents about the pregnancy and about Jeremy hitting her. They told her they would protect her, but she had to see this through. Kathleen would be a mom to a little baby boy in due time.

Jeremy came crawling back, apologizing and making empty promises about how he'd never touch her again like that and how he wanted to be a good father to his son. Kathleen's parents however, were skeptical and very resistant to let him anywhere near her or her unborn baby. He showed up with gifts for the baby, flowers, and anything else he could to help get back in Kathleen and her parents' good graces. Things improved, but only Kathleen let her guard down with Jeremy.

The night before a big chess meet that Kathleen and Camila were supposed to compete in, Kathleen was hanging out with Jeremy. She was supposed to be sleeping at Camila's that night and was headed there after she dropped off Jeremy, but when it came time to leave, he persuaded her to stay with him. Jeremy turned off the alarm when it went off the next morning and went back to sleep, never waking Kathleen. She woke up two hours late and missed the competition. That was the last time Camila spoke to Kathleen, not just because of the competition, but because she couldn't watch Kathleen ruin her life and was sick of being treated poorly. From that day forward, it was Jeremy and her unborn son and her parents. She never let anyone else in to her life.

Jeremy dropped out of school and Kathleen went into her Junior year about to give birth. She was homeschooled for most of her Junior year, until she was able to come back and graduate. Jeremy got a job at a gas station, then a fast food place, and then somewhere else. His temper didn't allow for him to be at a job very long— one inconvenience and he would blow up at his bosses. Jeremy and Kathleen got an apartment to raise their son, Drew. It wasn't till Drew was about two that Jeremy started coming home drunk and would get abusive to Kathleen. Drew would cry and beg daddy to stop and Jeremy would just glare and him and order him to get out.

The next morning when Jeremy left to go to work, Kathleen packed Drew's stuff and a few essentials and went back to her parents, begging for help. Her parents took them in as long as Kathleen stopped seeing Jeremy. This ended in many nights of the cops being called and Jeremy eventually was arrested for domestic violence and public intoxication. He ended up losing custody of Drew and Kathleen got a restraining order against him. This put Jeremy in a bad tailspin and he ended up involved in drugs and auto theft. Within the year, Jeremy was arrested, and was sent to jail for two-years.

During that time Kathleen went to college and got her prerequisites done for nursing school. She was about to start nursing school in the fall of that year. Drew would be four by then. She was excited, she felt she finally got her life back on track and Drew was happy and going to be starting kindergarten soon. She found a great part time job, working in a convalescent home as a maid, but quickly learned on the job and got trained as a CNA. She was a hard worker and smart, her compassion for the residents there was immeasurable. Everyone there loved Kathleen; this pushed her to pursue nursing even more.

About a month after Jeremy got released from jail, Kathleen ran into him at the store. He approached her as if he was a completely different person. Kathleen thought he had changed his ways. He went on and on about how life in prison made him a better man and he wanted a chance to be a good dad. He took her back to court to get visitation rights and due to his good behavior, the court obliged the request. Her parents were furious, but had no choice but to allow him to visit. They knew she would go back with him and sure enough Kathleen started to date Jeremy again.

One month later, Kathleen found herself pregnant with their second child. Her parents said they couldn't protect her anymore and wouldn't be here for her the next time she came running back. She always remembered her mother saying, "If he doesn't kill you first." No matter what Kathleen said, they didn't change their minds. Kathleen was heartbroken, losing someone else she loved. First her best friend and now her parents. She felt upset and misunderstood. She was doing the best she could for her family, but Kathleen found life to be very lonely. Jeremy was never home and Drew was in school. The weekends were the best, because she was with Drew. Drew was her life and Jeremy was becoming less and less of an attraction to her as she went through her pregnancy.

Although the physical abuse didn't come, he was mentally and emotionally abusive to Kathleen. She felt worthless when he would talk to her, he didn't appreciate her and he didn't care about their needs. They had a little girl, Amelia and they saved their money to buy a small house in Medford. The apartment was too cramped and expensive. Jeremy worked full time and was always pressuring Kathleen to pull her weight. So, Kathleen got a full time job at the convalescent home and dropped out of college. It wasn't the life she imagined but she loved her kids more than anything. Life was fine for the first two years back together, and Kathleen started to drop her guard. She thought Jeremy loved them, she thought they were a family. Her children having parents together was important, so she stayed and lived status quo life with Jeremy, they would work on their relationship eventually. Soon after Drew's sixth birthday party at the house, Jeremy started acting weird again, coming home late, drunk, and suddenly had money.

Kathleen waited up one night for him to come home, "Where have you been? I thought we were having dinner as a family tonight?" She started questioning him about his behavior and that was the last straw for Jeremy.

He snapped, "None of your business women. Know your place." Storming towards her. He hit Kathleen so hard that she couldn't go out in public because her eye was so black, blue, and swollen.

This was the beginning of the end for Kathleen. She stopped talking to him as her significant other. She would lock the bedroom door at night and the three of them would sleep together. One night it got so bad, she called the police and Jeremy got arrested. When he came back, he vowed to be different, repeating the same lies he always told her. Her love for her family blinded her and she always hoped this time would be different.

Drew started talking about his home life to his friends at school, and his friends got really scared for him. They went to their teacher, and the teacher went to the guidance counselor. After speaking to Drew themselves, Department of Children Services got involved. The kids were put in Kathleen's parents' custody until the investigation was concluded. The house was pristine, the kids had plenty of food, and were healthy. The case worker spoke to them both individually, and after everything was done, the case worker offered to help Kathleen if she felt in danger. Kathleen feared for her children and what Jeremy would do to retaliate if she was to tell the case worker the truth. So Jeremy and Kathleen pretended everything was great and Jeremy, for the fear of going back to prison, went back on his best behavior.

When Amelia turned five, her dad never showed to her big birthday party. She was devastated and Drew came and rocked her to sleep that night. "We don't need him, Amelia. He isn't worth your tears. Mom and I love you. He only hurts us." Kathleen's parents expressed their concern again to her, begging her to leave. Her parents took the kids for a sleepover and urged her to be sensible and pack their things. Kathleen cried herself to sleep that night, as Jeremy never came home. She decided to take a stand when he came home again. Kathleen was done being taken advantage of and being treated like a doormat.

The next day, Kathleen picked up Drew and Amelia. She sat them down in front of the TV with their lunch and told them to stay put so she could talk to daddy. Jeremy came home and Kathleen started on him about his behavior and how the police would take the children away from him if he didn't change his attitude. Jeremy's anger rose to new heights of cruelty. He beat Kathleen for the last time, thought she was dead, and planned to leave her that way. He looked at children watching TV and said, "I'm going to the gas station. When mom wakes up, tell her I'll be back." But he planned that she would never wake up and he would never return. Jeremy knew he would be back in prison this time if he stayed.

Drew and Amelia never saw him again. Amelia didn't remember, but Drew went to check on his mother and called 911 when he found her covered in blood on the floor of the bathroom. The police took them to their grandparents until Kathleen was strong enough to take them home. She was so happy that he didn't touch her children and left them alone. She tried to apologize to her parents, but they wouldn't answer and left her a note saying they couldn't help her anymore.

After that weekend, Kathleen never spoke to her parents again and her children never saw them again either. They told her it was too hard to deal with and they couldn't take the pain and worry of the next knock on the door being that their daughter was dead. Her parents moved away to Hawaii and that was the last time Kathleen saw her parents. Her parents both died of illness before Amelia's 10th birthday. Amelia never remembered them and Kathleen never talked about them. Drew would ask about them and Kathleen would lie to him, unable to tell him the painful truth. Eventually Drew stopped asking, but this pained Kathleen. She had lost every one of value in her life except her children and with that thought, she vowed to herself that she would never let anything come between her and her kids again.

Jeremy went back to prison for drug possession, domestic violence, and leaving a minor unsupervised. He was sentenced to 4 years in prison. Kathleen felt a sense of relief. She could start over and not live in fear of him coming back to finish her off. She filed a restraining order against him for when he got out and she vowed to never take him back. She had to do this for her children. Amelia would ask about where daddy was often, but over time, between Kathleen and Drew, she stopped. Drew would try and comfort Kathleen and tell her he was sorry for making him leave, but she always insisted that it wasn't Drew's fault. Jeremey had ruined her life and she wasn't going to let him ruin Drew's.

The pain and suffering Kathleen went through, because of her bad decisions, scarred her for life. She never dated again. She was constantly worried and tried to keep Drew and Amelia sheltered from her same mistakes. In fact, she used to tell Amelia she couldn't date till college. Kathleen only shared very small details about her past with Amelia, and Drew never mentioned to her about their dad being abusive. Kathleen was just thankful he never touched them. It made it easier for her to deal, because there is no greater pain than seeing your child suffer. She thanked god every day for that blessing, while also praying to keep them safe.

Kathleen ended up becoming a medical assistant and never went to nursing school. In 2011, when she was forty-nine years old, she was diagnosed with stage four kidney disease. The cancer had spread to her liver, bones, and brain. The hardest thing was how she couldn't tell Amelia right away, and didn't want to burden her with anything else until she was back. She would talk to her and visit and not tell her. It nearly killed her to lie to her, but she did what she thought was best. Kathleen hoped Amelia would understand one day. She ended up living out the rest of her days in the same convalescent home she worked in. She knew she couldn't beat the cancer so she lived on palliative treatments until she was placed on hospice.

Drew came home when she was first diagnosed and helped move her into the facility and said his goodbyes to her. He couldn't be away from work for that long and wanted Amelia and her to have time together without him being around to make it uncomfortable. Amelia would be back home soon and Drew wanted nothing to do with her. As much as it pained her to see her two children not speaking, she also didn't have the energy to argue and deep down knew they would eventually work it out. How could it not she thought, she prayed about it way too often for god not to answer her few prayers.

Jeremy moved out west when he got out of prison and never looked back. He didn't want to be a dad and the family life wasn't for him. He didn't want to risk going back to prison so he never even tried to see Kathleen again. He called for a couple of birthdays until Kathleen cut him off, saying they were better off with no contact as it was hard on the kids to only hear from him once a year. She told Jeremy he was violating the restraining order, and to lose their number, but in reality, it was hardest on Kathleen. She lived in fear he would come back and end up killing her or worse hurting her children. After that last call, she never heard from Jeremy again. She never knew if he was alive, dead, or back in prison, and as the years went on, the less she cared about it. Unfortunately, her fear for her kids' lives never left her.

Jeremy only thought about his children and Kathleen when he was trying to turn his life around and the thoughts were short and sweet. He spent his life drunk and in and out of homeless shelters. He would gamble and dabble in illicit activity until he ended up back in prison or homeless. This created a lot of enemies for Jeremy, as he owed a lot of people money. Jeremy never stayed put for too long and as he got older, tried to be smarter to avoid going back to prison. Jeremy's biggest problem was he was loud mouthed and impulsive, which usually lead to fighting and then fleeing from the police.

On February 4, 2014 at 3:57pm, Kathleen took her last breath. The final hours before cancer took Kathleen from this world was one of her best moments with Amelia. She for once was at peace, not living in pain or fear. She asked Amelia to promise her something before she died. The last thing she said to her was promise me you won't go looking for your father. For me, I love you, please don't look for him. It'll only bring you pain. As she held her hand, she took her last breathe and told Amelia she loved her. Amelia took those burdens with her, confusion and loneliness were two things that she constantly had, but she loved her mother and grew up knowing she was usually spot on with things. So Amelia promised her mother that she would carry out her wishes, including never seeking out Jeremy Pawsky.

Part One

Chapter 1

The sun shone down over a bed of flowers outside the Tuft

University classroom window. Inside the bright classroom sat 28-year-

old Amelia Pawsky, who was sitting for her last final examination

before graduation. With every gust of wind, Amelia could smell the

sweet fragrance of summer coming through the open window, and the

next chapter of her life which was about to begin. Amelia twisted her

long brown hair into a bun. She looked down at her exam and for the

next hour chewed her nails nervously as she worked through the

questions. Amelia's nails were unkempt, and her warm, beige skin

broken out from all the stress eating and makeup as she was looking to

relieve examination tension— but all that didn't matter anymore. She

made it through her last exam in this classroom, and in a few short days, she would officially be a Doctor of Veterinary Medicine. She was thankful that school was coming to an end, although focusing on her exams had been a great distraction from her dismal life. She definitely wasn't interested in a graduation ceremony. Amelia thought of the fact that no one cared about her or this accomplishment. She kept to herself mostly, only engaging with her classmates for assignments. She was a loner and preferred it that way, it was easier. Amelia knew she'd rather be on the road with Tune instead of being part of a ceremony. Tune, her 5-year-old dog, was the only constant thing in her life. She knew he would always be there.

She was beaming with excitement as she took her last stroll through the campus; her mood had significantly changed lately. She could finally escape Medford, Massachusetts and have a fresh start where no one knew her. People were always staring and silently judging Amelia for her past. The treacherous life of veterinary school meant a non-existent social and love life for her. Not that she liked to admit it, but she used school as an excuse to hide from others. As she walked through campus, she saw other students celebrating together. It was during times like this that Amelia wished she had someone to hang out with and celebrate, but she pushed everyone away after her last break up and never had any friends from her childhood after the accident. The thought of the accident had Amelia pull down her sleeves to hide the scars; the permanent tattoo on her body served as a reminder of the shames and secrets of her past.

Her break up with Elliot six months ago still weighed heavy on her mind; the constant thoughts of what she did wrong and where it went wrong were bottled deep down inside her. Elliot never did understand her and always wanted more from her. This left her feeling as she always felt, alone. Elliot always used to say, "You're so closed off, how can I get close to you when you won't let me in, or share anything with me?" Those were his last words to her before slamming the door, leaving her apartment, and walking out of Amelia's life forever. She hadn't heard from him since and the lack of closure burdened her to the extent that she was still not able to let go of so many unsaid feelings. No one ever cared about Amelia's view on things, it was like she didn't exist. She was used to that feeling, she thought to herself sadly.

As Amelia walked to her apartment, she thought about her mom's untimely death. Kathleen died at the young age of 52, and it was cancer that took her from Amelia. Amelia struggled with her mother's diagnosis, how she found out, and that it was kept from her for so long. But she knew why she did it and didn't want to spend the remaining time with her mom being upset. Amelia always had her mother, for her love was never-ending and pure; she always admired her mom's strength and kindness even with all that she endured in her lifetime. Amelia put her through so much agony and pain growing up, but she never wavered from her love for her children, Amelia and her brother, Drew. Amelia thought about her final hours with her mom, and even though it was full of sadness, there were no regrets. They laughed and cried together until her last breath.

Her mom made her promise to mend fences with Drew for her sake. Amelia couldn't deny her dying mother this wish, for it would be too cruel. She had no relationship with Drew, or any male in her life for that matter. The fact that her father, Jeremy, never cared about her and was never in her life burdened her with pain. She couldn't remember much about him and her mom refused to talk about her dad with her. And thanks to Drew's disappearing act, Amelia never got the closure she needed with the relationship. These thoughts entered her mind often, and in the end, left her with nothing but self-doubt.

Drew, of course, flew in and out the same day of the funeral. He'd left Massachusetts after the accident and blamed Amelia for ruining his life. Amelia, on the other hand, blamed herself for her mom inevitably losing her relationship with her son. She tried to make amends when he came home for their mother's burial, but he wouldn't have it. Drew wouldn't even look Amelia in the eyes; the feelings between them so tense that they could be cut with a knife. Matter of fact, she didn't even know where Drew lived, where he worked, and if he was in a serious relationship. She tried her best not to think of this though, because it only brought her more sadness.

About a month after Kathleen passed away, Amelia received a call from her mother's lawyer, Pete. Pete had presented Amelia with a letter explaining that it was necessary for him to keep it from Amelia until now because of Kathleen's wishes; she felt Amelia wouldn't be able to handle it immediately and wanted her to have time alone to grieve. After all, she was completely alone since her mother's death.

She had no one else's support. Amelia asked Pete if there was a letter left for Drew as well. But Pete said he couldn't say either way, upsetting her even more. *Why was everything always a secret?* The letter was simple: Amelia was to go to the provided address by noon the next day. Along with the address was a poem that her mom had written for her. But the very thought of it brought tears to her eyes and she'd never shared it with anyone; not even Elliot, who she dated for four years.

She still remembers pulling up to this house; it was a rainy and dreary March day as she got out of the car. Amelia was greeted by a woman who graciously welcomed her inside a barn off the side of her yard.

"My name is Eve, and these are my animals."

She was a middle-aged woman who seemed exhausted, and suddenly Amelia could see why. When they walked in, she was overwhelmed by the sight of dogs and cats. The lady looked at her and said, "Welcome to my rescue farm!"

Eve apologized for the abruptness of the situation and how she told Kathleen she didn't think it was a good idea to ambush Amelia. As Amelia looked around at all the animals, her heart melted. She loved animals and it was the only thing that made her happy lately. Her passion and her mother's drive for her to have a better life was what pushed Amelia to go to veterinary school. Confused as to whether this was a job interview or volunteer opportunity her mother set up for her, she abruptly started talking to Eve.

"What exactly is going on here? Why did my mom want me to come here?"

Eve looked at her with a nervous smile. "Come, he's right over here waiting for you."

Who is waiting for me she wondered as she followed Eve down the barn hallway. She could see dozens of animals all nestled in their homes that Eve must have built for them. Eve's work was amazing, like an angel's. *This would be heaven for me*, Amelia thought to herself. She walked along, taking in all the amazing animals and stopping to say hello. She was distracted on her way by a stunning, vibrant cardinal up on one of the beams.

Eve backtracked and asked, "Are you okay?" Amelia looked at Eve and pointed out her concern. Eve looked up and said, "You know that cardinal has been here since this morning." Amelia thought to herself that her mother must be with her here for this surprise. Eve took her by the hand. "Over here, this is what Kathleen picked out for you."

A beautiful three-month-old tan puppy was sleeping next to a cow. Eve looked at Amelia. "He is all yours!" she laughed. "Not the cow, just the pup! Go on and get acquainted," she gestured towards the puppy. There he was, all curled up. Amelia looked back at Eve, but she had already walked away.

Amelia remembers swooping down to scoop him up into her arms, thinking to herself... she now owned a dog. She'd never had a dog. *Can I do this?* Then she looked down at him, and he opened his eyes slightly and licked her chin. Amelia knew right then this was exactly what she needed and how he would end up probably rescuing her in the end. She sat there holding him for a while listening to the beautiful music in the background. It was at that moment that Amelia decided to name him Tune. She got up and took him to the pet store to get all that she needed for their new life. That was how Amelia got Tune; her best friend and savior. It was one of the best days of her life. This was exactly what mom was hoping for she thought to herself, as she entered her apartment and heard Tune barking and whacking his tail against the wall.

Chapter 2

Amelia took Tune for his evening walk while she listened to a podcast to help her study for the national exam. It was on different cases to help her prepare for any situation that could arise. She was currently listening to a case about a dog getting attacked by a snake. The most important thing to take from this case was the key symptoms the dog would exhibit and marks to look out for. This was to determine if the snake was venomous or not. Amelia was intrigued by reptiles and opted to take an extra course about the species in her last semester. She planned to open her own veterinary hospital and her own rescue and was eager to start fresh somewhere new with Tune. She always imagined the rescue to be a big blue building with enough land to give the animals room to roam on the same property as her home. In the city, Amelia would have a veterinary clinic called "Wags to

Whimpers" to care for animals' everyday needs, like wellness

examinations and small issues. Her examination was in a few days,

and she couldn't wait to get started on her new business venture. After

Friday, she would be packing up and moving to California. She would

drive, because the sheer thought of putting Tune on a plane gave her

anxiety; plus it would give them time to sightsee. The only thing she'd

miss about this state was visiting her mom's grave, but she'd come

back, she thought to herself quickly, not wanting to dwell on it.

As the week went by, she packed up the little that she wanted

to take with her. This equated to one box. Tune had more things than

she did, and that was fine by her. Amelia studied till she couldn't stand

it anymore, patiently waiting for Friday to come. It seemed like the

week dragged on slowly. She woke up early that day to work out

before her examination; trying to clear some of the anxiety and

pressure that was building up. Today was the first day of her new

journey, and their new life.

She took her national licensing examination; it took about four

hours before the screen popped up to notify her, *passed!* The relief that

flooded Amelia's eyes as she drove to her mom's grave was a mixture of the last few years, of being completely alone and working incredibly hard. She parked in the same spot she always did every Friday for the last five years. As she walked up to visit her mother, she cried happy tears, and her cheeks flushed with color as she pressed her hand on her gravestone, "I did it momma, I promised you I'd make you proud." She sat there on the ground in front of her talking about the last week, convincing herself more than anything that she would be back to visit soon. She cleaned the grave one last time before placing a single sunflower, her mother's favorite, on the top on the tombstone, saying her last goodbye for a while. She got up and walked over to another gravestone, apologized and prayed, before walking back to her car. She sat there in silence and gained composure before leaving to get Tune. They'd be on the road soon enough, away from all the bad memories Massachusetts held for Amelia.

Amelia came home to grab Tune and then set off on their journey. She looked in the rearview mirror one last time as she drove away. This apartment had been her safe haven for five years after she settled Kathleen's' estate, sold the house, and anything she and Drew didn't want. She would move into her own place, it was too hard to live there. Everywhere she looked reminded Amelia of her painful childhood, and her mom. Amelia's dad, Jeremy, had walked out that door when she was five years old to go to the gas station, and he never came back. That was the last time she saw Jeremy, he attempted to call a few times over the years, but it became too painful for everyone, especially for her mom. The tears, pain, and secrets those house walls held were enough to make Amelia never want to return. She looked through the rearview mirror at the cardboard box sitting on the back seat. It held the few items from her childhood that were important to her— a couple of pictures, a baseball glove, a necklace, and folder of papers. *Pathetic how twenty-eight years of life could be summed up in a single box*, she thought, and in that moment, Tune licked her cheek and snapped her out of it. He was good at giving her a reason to smile. She brushed off those feelings, looked forward, grabbed Tune's paw, and asked, "Are you ready to go on an adventure, Tune butt!?"

He cocked his head side to side and wagged his tail against the door, barked gently and rubbed his forehead against the side of her face. Amelia giggled. "I love you too Tuney!" as she put the car in drive and took off.

Amelia sang, and danced for the first few hours, because of the excitement surrounding her passing the national exam, and road tripping with Tune. Tune kept looking at her like she was crazy, before staring back out the window. Amelia was always singing and talking to him in her special voice that she used when talking to animals. Even though she believed that he loved it and his nicknames, she found herself feeling self-conscious about it from time to time because Elliot used to make fun of her for talking to Tune. "You know he's just a dog right? You're so weird. You look stupid when you talk like that." She could still hear him say these things in her head, it made her feel, just as she always felt— alone and misunderstood.

After a few hours, she pulled over to get gas and some food. Tune got out and ran around for a few minutes, before they were back on the road. Amelia drove till about 10pm that night, until she couldn't keep her eyes open anymore. She decided to get off the highway and get a motel room for the night in Pennsylvania. It wasn't the most glamorous of places, but they allowed dogs, and the rate was decent.

Amelia was so happy to sleep in a queen size bed. The two of them could finally stretch out and have plenty of room to sleep! Tune paced back and forth for two hours before settling down in bed to cuddle with Amelia. He loved to be under the covers, which was fine with Amelia because she was always cold. Amelia tried to calm her mind, she had to get some sleep, but her mind kept racing. She found herself thinking of the time when Elliot surprised her and took her away for the weekend. That was the last time she was in a hotel room. The weekend had ended abruptly because of the same old argument of Amelia being too closed off, and how his friends thought she was nuts and weird. They packed up, headed back to her apartment, and that was when Elliot left her forever. The thought of this memory made her tear up. She had to put on some white noise on her phone, to help clear her head, and the next thing she knew, she passed out. The next day they would continue on their journey west.

The morning was uneventful. Amelia walked Tune and couldn't stop thinking of Californian sunshine. Once they got back to the hotel, she checked out the almost inedible free breakfast. The eggs looked like they were from a fast food place, and the orange juice and apple juice looked the same. Amelia raised her eyebrows, grabbed a stale bagel, coffee, and some eggs for Tune. Tune didn't seem to mind though, he thought he was getting a treat. She got in the car to start it up, but it took a few attempts. She knew her Toyota Corolla was getting old— it did have over 200,000 miles on it and all— but she rubbed the dash, "Come on girl, we got this" and went on her way.

Tune was all curled up, sleeping next to her as she drove, nudging her arm and licking her every now and then wanting pats, which she happily gave him. They stopped a few times to eat, use the bathroom, and to stretch their legs. Tune loved to play fetch, so Amelia stopped by an empty field to help him work off some of his pent up energy. He was still a puppy, and full of excitement. Tune had never been on a road trip before and wasn't used to not being able to roam around freely.

Amelia had gotten off the highway to stop for the night after she saw a motel sign that said pet-friendly underneath. The drive was going fine till then; it was about 8 o'clock in the evening when the road trip started to get interesting. Amelia was driving along this road with fields of corn on either side of them for what seemed like forever. It was dark, there were barely any street lights, and she found herself dozing off. When she opened her eyes back up, she slammed her foot on the brakes. She was staring at a deer on the road and was about to have a head-on collision. She swerved the car hard to the left and tried to slow down to stop, but the tire blew and the car to swerved even more. Amelia felt the car as it started to spin towards a ravine. She couldn't get control of the car, panic started setting in, and she slammed on her brakes harder, and screamed as the car flipped. All Amelia remembered was grabbing Tune and bracing herself for the crash that was about to happen.

Amelia opened her eyes in a panic and looked for Tune, but she could barely see. She heard Tune whimpering behind her, and Amelia yelled out for him, crying and apologizing. He was stuck between the seat and the floor of the car. The car was smoking, and her left leg was bleeding and burning with pain. Amelia thought that her leg was broken and she couldn't move it, but she needed to move to save Tune. She was disorientated from the impact of the crash, and blood was trickling down her face from a gash on her forehead. She thought the car was on its front end in the ravine but couldn't see anything beyond the smoke billowing out of the hood of the car. Tune was stuck too; Amelia didn't want to move her seat because she didn't want to risk hurting Tune any more than he was already. The hood of the car caught fire, and she screamed in pain as she forced her leg out of the wedge between the car door and the steering wheel. Amelia tried very hard to move towards Tune. The car was filling up with smoke and burning Amelia's eyes but she didn't care, she just wanted to be with Tune. He whimpered and licked her hand as she reached for him, thinking this was it for them. The pain and blood loss was winning over Amelia's consciousness, she could feel the anxiety rising in her. A flashback of her past was rushing into her mind, and she started screaming. She thought she heard Tune bark, but it seemed so far away.

Chapter 3

Amelia woke up in a foreign place and was struggling to recall her last memory. She started blinking fast and tried to sit up, but she was encumbered with pain. Her heart was racing when she heard a man's voice say, "it is okay, try to remain calm, and I'll explain everything." The man came and sat down next to her bed to comfort her, reaching out to grab her hand. "My name is Teddy, I have your dog. He is safe." The man's voice was so calm and reassuring.

Amelia was straining to get her eyes to focus on the man standing in front of her. She looked at the man for what seemed like a long time then said, "Where am I? Who are you?" "Tune, where's Tune?" "Is he okay?" Amelia's heart was pounding, and the alarm started sounding in her room, nurses came rushing in, and everything became foggy again. She tried so hard to stay awake, but the darkness consumed her.

Amelia woke up to what seemed like people talking all around her. "She suffered a lot of trauma to her body with that crash, and it was going to take her a while to recover. Teddy are you sure you want to stay again? It has been three days already," she heard the nurse say.

Teddy sleepily replied, "Yes, I'm staying, I'll go home to feed the animals and come back after I shower. I'm not leaving this woman all alone. She has no one."

Amelia wondered how this Teddy person could know anything — what accident? Before she could get any answers, she fell back asleep. *Why can't I wake up* she worried, drifting back into this dark place she called life. She had to find Tune, she needed to wake up. He needed her, and she also needed him.

It wasn't until her fifth day in the hospital that she regained full consciousness to talk to a doctor. She listened while he examined her. Dr. Rhine introduced himself and told Amelia that she had been in a bad car accident and suffered major damage to her left leg and arm.

She had hit her head pretty hard, creating a concussion. Dr. Rhine

asked her some questions about who she was, to get an idea of her

mental state of mind. All Amelia wanted to know was where Tune was.

Dr. Rhine stated he wasn't sure of the condition or whereabouts of her

dog. Amelia broke down crying, she was inconsolable; the doctor

couldn't understand anything she was saying because she was crying

so hard and was losing control of her breathing. He begged her,

"please try to calm down; otherwise, I'll have to sedate you!"

Dr. Rhine was concerned with how she was moving around

erratically; he didn't want her to self-inflict any more traumas to her

body. Amelia wasn't hearing any of this as a flashback of the crash

came rushing into her mind.

It was smoky in the car, she could hear Tune as she was trying

to talk to him and reach for him, but her leg was stuck, and creating

excruciating pain. Tune, Tune I'm coming, then a fire broke out, and

glass hit her face with a wave of heat. Tune started barking like crazy

and whimpering, it was like he was trying to move free. Amelia was

struggling with her own flashbacks as they came flooding back in, as if

it was yesterday. The trauma from the car accident triggered her agony from the worst day of her life, then a man's voice in the distance calling out, trying to help. "Who's this man who saved us?"

That was all she could remember because everything was going dark again. Was this a dream? She thought. *I just need to wake up*, she told herself. *Come on Amelia wake up*, but nothing happened, it was still dark and groggy.

She could faintly hear the man, Teddy, talking to her it seemed. Reaching for her hand and whispering to her "Amelia wake up please, Tune misses you!"

Tune she thought, *he's okay, he's alive*. Relieved she fell back into a deep sleep.

Amelia remained in and out of consciousness days, saying no more than a word here or there then falling right back into her stupor. She finally woke up on day seven to two men arguing. "It isn't normal for her to still be out, she should have woken up by now. How much did you sedate her?"

The other man was getting irritated. "She was having too much movement to her leg; if we aren't careful, she might not regain full function of her leg. My goal is to keep her calm until her mind and body can heal enough to deal with this trauma."

Amelia was groggy, and her voice was croaking from lack of use. "What's wrong with my leg?"

The two men rushed over to her. "Hey, there you are! I was getting worried about you!" Teddy said urgently.

Amelia was confused. "I heard you saying that, but do I know you?"

Dr. Rhine cut in. "You can talk with Teddy later, we need to talk about some other important things first okay?"

Amelia nodded to Dr. Rhine as he reintroduced himself, and then went into details about her extensive injuries. Amelia learned that her leg was crushed, her nerves were compromised, and she was in a brace with pins sticking out of her leg to try and stabilize it. She looked down at her legs, the left one suspended in a leg rest about four inches off the bed. She had two surgeries in the past week on her leg and arm. With her leg, Dr. Rhine explained, it will require at least one more surgery to remove the pins and place a metal rod before a cast would be put on. The doctor explained that this was necessary if she hoped to walk again; hearing this, Amelia cried silently, tears flowing down her face. Teddy handed her a napkin and went on to grab her hand when Amelia jerked it away and stared at him.

He jumped back and apologized. "I was only trying to comfort you." Amelia didn't understand that at all. She hadn't had comfort for a long time.

The doctor left her with some paperwork and said he'd be back tomorrow. The paperwork had to be about 30 pages long. She couldn't even fill them out, because she couldn't hold a pen.

Teddy interrupted her thoughts. "You're left-handed?" He has a worried smile on his face, as if he was waiting for her to lash out again.

She looked at him puzzled for a few seconds."Yes, why?" she said, her eyebrows raising with annoyance.

He looked at her pitifully as he said, "If you'd like, I can help you."

Amelia grudgingly thanked him as he grabbed the clipboard full of papers. She looked away feeling ashamed and confused. *Why was this man being so nice to her? Why does he seem to care about her? He doesn't even know me*.

Teddy sat forward to grab the clipboard from Amelia and started asking her questions from the form. She found herself staring at him as she answered. Teddy was so intriguing to her, it was like she was in a trance. Gravitating towards a complete stranger, Amelia wanted so badly to be held. She regretted being mean and yelling at him for touching her earlier. These feelings were foreign to Amelia that it made her nervous. She immediately started to wonder what he thought he would get out of this. She decided to start asking him questions.

Amelia found out through Teddy that she would be leaving soon if she stayed stable. She would be transferred to a rehabilitation center in three days since she didn't live there or have anyone to care for her. The thought of living somewhere like that immediately made her think of Tune and what she would do for him while she was in the facility healing.

She just sat there and cried, wishing she could hold Tune. Tune, she thought and looked at Teddy. "Do you know where Tune is? My dog!" she asked panicked.

Teddy looked up from the clipboard at her, "It is okay, he's safe and recovering at my farm."

"What!?" she stammered, "what's wrong with him?" She started to breathe heavily.

Teddy explained that Tune had a couple of burn marks and some deep cuts, but he would make a full recovery and seemed to be in decent spirits. He said all of this so calmly and was very kind about it that it was making Amelia feel uneasy again.

"He's always looking for you though. I would like to bring you to see him as soon as I can," Teddy said. In shock, she stared at him, and Teddy replied with a warm smile to try to give her some ease. "He's with Sapphire, and he's not alone. He's okay, I think they really like being with each other." Teddy reached out to touch her hand and then remembered and recoiled.

Amelia noticed this at once, and reached her hand out to meet his as she closed her eyes. She silently hoped he would reach out and hold her hand. Teddy smiled and took her hand, moving closer to her bedside with his chair and with that, Amelia let out a sigh of relief, thankful that Tune was okay. She mustered enough energy to ask Teddy to take her today. "Please, I need him, and he needs me." Exhaustion was setting in.

Teddy said, "I'll talk to Dr. Rhine, and see what I can do. You need to rest, so you can get better for Tune." As he got up and placed the clipboard on her side table. "We can finish this later." looking down at her as he stood up, flushed cheeks and smiling.

Amelia nodded. "Thank you for saving us, I don't know how I'll repay you." As she slowly closed her eyes and laid back, the next thing Teddy knew, she was out cold.

Amelia was in full mom mode that she forgot that she was a vet for a second, and couldn't seem to comprehend Tune's condition besides that Teddy thought he was okay. She blamed this on the head trauma and the pain pills. As she drifted off to sleep, her last thought was, *he's a dog person, and Tune is in good hands*.

Over the next few days, Amelia was taken downstairs for many tests and appointments with different doctors to see how she was mentally and physically. She had the final surgery for her leg, and they placed a cast on it all the way to her hip. It was so uncomfortable and itchy but felt more stable and wasn't as painful. Teddy came every day with updates about Tune and to sit with her. They talked, but not too much; she just kept asking Teddy to see the pictures of Tune and Sapphire over and over. She used this as motivation to push through her treatments and tests. Amelia was so exhausted that she would fall asleep listening to Teddy talk or hum. In fact, after him being here with her for well over a week, she didn't know much about him at all. Didn't he work, have a family or need to be anywhere else? She found this very weird, did she even want this man being here all the time? Amelia decided to not say anything, for whatever reason he was taking care of Tune and she needed someone for him.

A few days later, Amelia started to cry out of frustration and missing Tune. She was thankful that Teddy was there to talk to, but she missed holding Tune and loving on him. Amelia wanted so badly to just cuddle, she was lonely and in need of physical affection. In the moment of her crying, Teddy came over and immediately sat on the bed next to her to comfort her. When she looked up at him, she asked, "Will you lay down with him, I miss Tune and I'm feeling so lonely."

Teddy didn't even hesitate, lying beside her with his arm around her, humming to her as she calmed down. Teddy immediately passed out from exhaustion. Amelia couldn't believe how natural it felt, and she immediately felt at ease. She felt Teddy get up a while later, gently brushing her hair out of her face and covering her back up with a blanket. As he bent down to kiss her forehead, he whispered, "Going to see Sapphire and Tune, will be back later." And off he went. She feel back asleep smiling, hoping he was not a dream.

On Monday morning, Teddy showed up and offered to drive her to the rehabilitation center. She debated with him for a good five minutes about not wanting to trouble him. There was definitely tension between them after the previous day of cuddling. Amelia couldn't decide if she wanted to yell at him or jump him right then and there. He was very adamant and pushy, which was annoying and attractive at the same time. Amelia was even more irritated with herself for feeling this way for someone she barely knew. She had met a million people, what made him so special?

As doctor walked away, Amelia heard him mumbling, "These two are like a married couple, figure it out already."

They both blushed and started laughing. Amelia hung her head and slapped her hands on her knees. It felt good to laugh again. Teddy handed her coffee, and she melted. She hadn't had a decent cup of coffee in forever, but quickly changed her facial expression since she didn't want him to see her that way. Amelia hated how closed off she could be sometimes.

It was the first time Amelia laughed in a while or felt any type of happiness, she realized as he wheeled her out to his truck. Teddy helped her into this older Ford pick-up truck. It was red with a white strip down the sides. His truck was pretty clean, she thought as Teddy started to drive away from the hospital. It was like every minute that passed she found more and more things that she liked about the man who dropped everything to help her. Amelia started to feel

uncomfortable and with knowing what to do, stared out the window.

Chapter 4

Being in the truck with someone she barely knew seemed to be bothering her much more than she anticipated, but maybe it was also the fear of living in a rehabilitation center too. She had never allowed herself to be *taken care of* by anyone else before. Despite Amelia's efforts, she couldn't do anything alone over the last two days. She knew she needed the help; she couldn't even go to the bathroom alone. Tune and her mother were the only people who saw her vulnerability. Ever since she was in a juvenile delinquent facility, she learned to hide all emotions and to be vigilantly display a strong exterior.

She decided to distract herself by looking through the mounds of paperwork she was given, but it started to make her nauseous. Just when she decided to reluctantly start a conversation with Teddy, his phone rang.

He apologized and answered, "What? You know I'm busy with Amelia… what slow down, I can't understand you." All Amelia could hear was loud crying and screaming-like sounds; she knew something bad was going on. She stared at Teddy and watched the color leave his face as he said, "I'll be there in five minutes, keep her calm, put her with Tune."

He hung up and whipped the truck in the opposite direction and started driving like crazy. Amelia was screaming all of a sudden, emotions were rising in both of them and she was starting to have a flashback but pushed it out to yell at him to find out what was wrong. Amelia tried to brace herself as best as she could with one arm and leg, but it was useless.

Teddy yelled, "You can't do anything anyway, so just be quiet, and let me think." She stared in disbelief, listening and watching his expressions. He was mumbling, "Snake, how the hell, a snake, no she has to be wrong."

Amelia looked at him and said, "Did Sapphire get bit by a snake?"

He looked at her and shouted, "Yes, now be quiet!" But before he could finish, Amelia shut him up.

"I'm a veterinarian, take me there now! Call back whoever that was and see if they know anything about the snake and tell them not to touch that wound." Amelia said in a panicked tone.

Teddy did as instructed, starring big-eyed at her, calling back the woman to find out more information. Teddy relayed the information back to Amelia and by the time he gave her all the details they were there, Amelia knew that she couldn't diagnose the dog's condition or know if the snake was venomous until she saw the wound.

He ran around the truck, threw open the truck door and carried her to his dog, Sapphire. She looked at him in disbelief but knew it wasn't the time or place to argue. Amelia looked at Sapphire and talked to her soothingly as she lightly wagged her tail on the floor. She examined the wound on her hind leg near her right hip. The area was bright red, and the tissue was already swelling, but the multiple bite marks were not the evidence of a venomous snake, and this made

Amelia feel relieved. *It'll bruise, but I'll clean it out and watch for infection* she thought to herself. Teddy stayed on the other side of the room with Tune and waited for her instruction. She could hear Tune whimpering and was dying to see him. It had been weeks since Amelia had held her dog and she couldn't wait.

She finally called out, "It's okay. She's going to be okay because it wasn't poisonous. I just need to clean it up and wrap it, she's going to be sore but will recover fully. There must be a nest nearby where she was attacked. I'd clear it out if I were you. Looks like maybe a king or rat snake; are they common here in Indiana?" she asked as she turned to look over her shoulder at Teddy.

Teddy stared at her for a while before he spoke with watery eyes and crooked voice. "Can I see her now?"

Amelia felt this was the first time she really saw him. His emotions were so raw and real, something Elliot never exhibited when she was with him. This was a trait Amelia admired the most of Teddy so far. The fact that he was an animal lover tugged at her heart strings.

She shook her head to clear her thoughts, and she answered, "Yes of course and I'd love to finally hold Tune."

Teddy smiled and walked over with Tune to Amelia and Sapphire. The four of them sat in a circle holding each other; as Amelia knew all too well, things could have gone so much worse for both Teddy and her over the last two weeks.

This was why she became a vet, she thought. This moment right here. Tune was alive and recovering, Sapphire was going to be perfectly fine after being on the mend for a week or so. She reached over and grabbed Teddy's hand for a few minutes as they locked eyes. Teddy gently brought his head towards her, and sighed what seemed like relief. Amelia looked up at Teddy and he reacted, Teddy gently wiped her tears from her cheeks and kissed her so softly and passionately that Amelia felt dizzy. She responded to his touch and pulled Teddy towards her, yearning for more. Teddy let out a soft moaning sound and pushed himself towards her, trying to be careful of her leg and arm. Amelia pulled him close and put her head into his shoulder, as he gently rocked back and forth, holding each other. Tune, licked Amelia's hand and she pet Tune's head as she lifted sat back up.

Then, suddenly it was like they both realized what was going on, and recoiled from each other. They brought all their attention back to Sapphire and Tune, who had patiently been waiting for belly rubs. She didn't know what made her want to impulsively be physical with Teddy, but for the first time in a long time, she felt something for someone else other than Elliot.

After Amelia and Tune had their reunion, she went into full vet mode and started examining his injuries. Tune's wounds appeared clean and were starting to heal; the dressings on his ribs seemed decent but needed to be redone. He looked great, his color was good, his temperature seemed fine, and he was eating well. Amelia was generally pleased with how he had healed over the past few weeks while she was in the hospital.

"What kind of medicine has he been receiving?" she asked Teddy, peering up at him from the top of her eyes without losing sight of Tune.

He looked over at her and blushed, "I've only been using supplies here, Neosporin and bandages. I'm sorry; I've been concentrating on you over the last few weeks because I thought he was okay." Teddy looked sheepish, and Amelia immediately felt bad for even implying she wasn't grateful.

Amelia looked at him and said, "No, no he's fine. I really appreciate it. I have some burn cream for animals in my vet bag in my car. Do you know if anything was salvageable, or what condition my car is currently in?"

At that moment, a woman came in and asked, "How is she doing? Teddy, I can bring you out to where I found Sapphire."

Teddy looked at her and introduced Amelia. "This is Rhoda, she works here at the vineyard."

Amelia smiled and said, "Hello, nice to meet you."

Teddy asked if they could have this conversation later and Amelia nodded, then turned her attention back to Tune. She couldn't help but react to what Teddy said about a vineyard. How did she not notice that pulling up? She blamed it on the chaos of the moment and returned her full attention to Tune.

Amelia met up with Teddy an hour or so later. Teddy had a bag that he was carrying over to her and it was moving. She knew instantly that he had found the nest. Her veterinary side was itching to be used as she eagerly reached her hands out to him. She couldn't move, and this was getting more and more aggravating by the minute. Tune had already bumped her leg and arm unfavorably multiple times. She was going to need medication and a more secure place to hunker down in so she could relax for a while. This was the most excitement she had in weeks since the accident and it was wearing her down.

Teddy was approaching her and, as though he could see the excitement and the pain in her eyes, he stopped dead in his tracks. "I shouldn't have done this to you today, I'm so sorry. How is the pain?"

Amelia blew him off with a wave of her hand "Let me see the snake? Did you find any eggs? Where was she hiding?"

He mumbled how stubborn she was and approached anyway. "Well then, she is not happy that she is trapped in this bag, please be careful. I didn't even think to look for eggs, she was hard to trap, very aggressive when I cornered her. Makes sense now!"

Amelia looked up at him. "Can you get me a nice size tank for us to keep her? I can set up a nice home for her and her eggs. They really are nice reptiles when not provoked or feeling endangered. They don't like to be cornered, and she was protecting her eggs."

Teddy looked at her, amazed. "You want to keep her here? She just attacked Sapphire, aren't you worried?" His temper seemed to be rising at the memory.

"I'm too exhausted to argue about this. Please, just get what I need, we don't have to keep her forever. I'm fascinated by them and want to learn from them. It's kind of my job, and I took extra classes in college that specializes in reptiles."

"As long as the other animals are safe, then fine, but this is only temporary for now," he agreed reluctantly, shaking his head as he left to get what she requested. "I'm leaving the bag tied in the back of the pickup till I get back." Teddy walked back out to go look for the eggs.

She nodded as she continued to do research on her phone, looking up how long mother snakes could stay together in the same tank, how to check the sex of a snake. It could be very tricky, and they couldn't stay together, if they were the same sex and are adults, they will attack each other. She found out that once she lays the eggs, it takes about 2 months. She was pretty certain he would find anywhere from 10-20 eggs. Amelia learned this was an endangered species of snake too; Grey Rat snakes were mostly common in Canada but have been commonly found in Indiana.

Teddy came back with a shoebox and the bag. "I can't believe it, good thing you made me go back, 13 eggs! I have them in here." He handed over the shoebox to her.

She gasped with excitement and opened the lid to examine them immediately. She explained to Teddy that she was in fact a grey rat snake, how she'd need some wood chips, and branch. Lastly, a heat lamp or heat pad to provide the best element for them. "Once you get all of this, we will place the eggs first, before you put her in, she is going to be very protective of her eggs. We can just cut a hole in the top of the box for her to get to her eggs and keep them protected," she said.

He shook his head and left mumbling, "snakes, seriously caring for the snakes that attacked my dog."

As she waited, Tune and Sapphire cuddled by her side, occasionally lifting their heads to lick her hands. She was recounting the whole snake conversation and couldn't believe she said "we." Why was she having "we" conversations with a man she barely knew? She was losing it, she tried to blame it on the medications, but she also knew it wasn't true. Teddy seemed too good to be true. What was his secret, why is he alone? She asked herself these questions and then thought better of it. She wasn't ready to have this conversation with herself, so she went back to obsessing over the snakes. She was researching again on her phone when Teddy came back with everything that was needed.

Amelia yelled, "Be careful, I can do it if you want, I don't want her to bite you." Teddy waved her off and set up the enclosure as she instructed. Amelia mentioned how they ate rats. Teddy smiled. "There are tons of rats around, so it won't be a problem."

Luckily for Amelia, Teddy's sister used to own an iguana, and he brought out this huge tank that it used to live in years ago. It was a 15-gallon tank, which was perfect. Teddy placed her in the tank and Amelia took a closer look. She was gorgeous about 5 feet long, it had grey and brown horizontal stripy blotches.

As she watched him set everything up, she found herself starring endlessly at him. He was definitely attractive, and it aroused a sense of excitement in her. His butt did look nice in those jeans, she smirked to herself. She couldn't believe her own behavior and forcing herself to focus on Tune and Sapphire was harder than she thought. He seemed to be a good man, caring, loving, and nurturing; even to a snake that bit his dog. She found herself envisioning a life with him and a family until she was interrupted by his humming. It had snapped her out of her own thoughts and she listened and smiled as he moved back in forth to his own rhythm.

"So, my car, what's its status?" Amelia awkwardly blurted out.

He looked back at her sadly. "It's totaled, and all the cops were able to salvage was one box, but it's in rough shape.

He apologized to her as he saw her face drop. Amelia had received the vet bag as a gift from her mother right before she died. Amelia was torn about this, but was thankful for Tune's safety, and realized that the vet bag could be replaced. She kicked herself for not wearing the necklace, praying that it was repairable. The necklace was her grandmothers', the only heirloom she ever passed to Amelia. It was a gold locket with a sapphire gem in the center of the oval and unique design engraved in it.

"Do you know about the necklace in the box?" Amelia croaked.

Teddy looked over his shoulder at her "I'll go to the police tomorrow and collect the box for you to go through." She thanked him and then went completely silent, thinking about her mother while rubbing Tune's head.

After all the excitement, the pain was getting to her, and she found herself whimpering out loud before she could stop herself, causing Teddy to come running over. She stared at him; he was a good looking man, tall 6' man with olive skin, dressed in flannel and weathered blue jeans.

"That's it, you're going inside, let me get you some food, and we have to figure out your arrangements," Teddy said sternly.

Before she could argue, Teddy swept her up in his muscular arms and carried her inside his house. She found herself completely content being in his arms with her head resting on his chest. Amelia had never felt like this with Elliot, and the feelings overwhelmed her. How hard did she hit her head? This has to be all from the medications she thought trying to shake off her feelings for Teddy. He took a deep breath as he lowered his chin, resting it on her head, he started to hum, and Amelia felt herself fall into a blissful state of contentment that overcame her.

The butterfly tingling feeling in the pit of Amelia's stomach left her wanting more. Teddy laid her down on his bed, covering her with a blanket, her lingering eyes falling upon his face. He looked down at her, his hazel eyes piercing through her. His confidence and strong gaze was so attractive that Amelia couldn't help herself. As Teddy bent down to whisper to her, Amelia reached up to graze his face with her fingers, then cupped her hand around his neck, guiding his lips towards hers. He willingly succumbed to her touch as he passionately kissed her, gently rubbing his fingers along her spine.

As Teddy slowly pulled away, he whispered "I'll be back with food for you and your medications.

Amelia smiled at Teddy as he sat up. Nodding her head, as she watched him walk away, before she closed her eyes, and fell into a deep sleep. She couldn't remember the last time she felt safe and happy.

Chapter 5

Amelia woke a few hours later to Tune licking her face, a plate with a sandwich, a glass of water, and her medications, accompanied by a little note scribbled, '*You were sleeping so soundly, I didn't want to wake you. Ring the bell when you need me.*' Amelia rolled her eyes at this, but couldn't help smiling and think of how sweet this was in her mind.

She reluctantly did as instructed, only because she desperately needed to use the bathroom. She ate her sandwich and took her pills, eagerly waiting for the medication to set in. The pain was bad, just too much excitement as she recounted the morning. She looked at her phone, it was four o'clock in the afternoon; wasn't she supposed to be at Vine Stay Rehabilitation Center? Why weren't they calling wondering where she? She rang the bell gritting her teeth. *How juvenile, why couldn't he leave me his number to text?*

Teddy came running in, smiling, "You're up! How are you feeling?" His sleeves were rolled up and he wiped his hands on a dish towel.

She looked at him and melted inside, but stayed stern in her response. "Not great, why am I not at the rehab place? Why haven't they called looking for me? Why am I here Teddy?" Amelia wanted him to tell her he wanted her to stay, but it came out way harsher than she meant. *Of course he's not going to say that* she thought to herself. *You're an idiot Amelia.* Regret immediately set in.

He looked at her in shock, stumbling over his words, "You were in so much pain and needed rest, I'm sorry, you told me to bring you here when you heard about Sapphire, I'll take you there now" he said, trailing off, turning red and walking away before Amelia could even respond.

Teddy came back a few minutes later, red in the face, "Are you ready?" looking down at his feet.

"Yes." Amelia said quietly looking abashed.

Teddy picked her up and carried her to the truck, Amelia felt how tense he was holding her and she felt even worse. She could tell how upset she made him by her outburst.

In the truck, Amelia felt bad. What was wrong with her? She tried to apologize, "Teddy, I'm..."

Teddy cut her off. "Don't bother, it was my fault. You can go back to being alone at the rehab place. I'll watch Tune till you are released." Teddy wouldn't even look at her as he drove staring straight out at the road.

Amelia realized that, for the first time in her life, she had other people in her life to be considerate of. She was no longer a one-woman band with a beloved loyal dog.

She sat there, not knowing what to do or say, her temper rising. *How could he not understand? Why does he care so much? Why won't he let me be?* Anger and fear of the unknown slowly escalated in her.

What am I going to do at rehab? Who will I live with? What kind of

conditions? What will I eat? How will I pay for this? How long will

they keep me? She couldn't contain it anymore and exploded with

emotion.

She started to cry. "Please stop the car. PLEASE!" She

screamed a bunch of nonsense. He pulled over saying, "Calm down, I

can't understand you!" When that didn't seem to work, he decided to

pull her into a hug to try and calm her down. Her resistance was strong

for a few moments, and then she coiled into a ball on his chest,

sobbing uncontrollably, "Alone…. mom…. no one… died….Tune."

This lasted a good five minutes, before she sat up, took a deep breath,

and started to wipe her face and blow her nose. She then looked out

the window when she went to apologize to Teddy, not wanting him to

see the look on her face.

"I'm sorry you had to witness that, I don't know what's wrong

with me lately. I'm never this emotional. I don't know what to say,

thank you for everything you've done for Tune and me… strangers to

you. Thank you." The rambling continued for a while and then she could feel herself turning red she looked down at her hands, for fear of meeting his eyes. *He must think I'm a train wreck.*

Teddy reached out to her hand and squeezed it, "Look at me, Amelia."

Nothing happened for what seemed like a long time. Then she turned with tears silently streaming down her face. He reached up and wiped them away.

"I want you to stay with me if you'd like. I can bring you to and from therapy when you have appointments, and you can stay with Tune in our guest house if you'd be more comfortable. I don't know what it is about you, but from the moment I saw you, I've just been pulled towards you like a magnet." He looked surprised. "I can't believe I just said that, but it's true. I know we haven't known each other long," he said, staring at her abashed.

Amelia impulsively reached over to pull him towards her, grabbing his shirt. Teddy responded immediately, coming over to her, reaching up to move her hair off her face, then gently bringing his lips to meet hers. The sparks were flying, kissing passionately, Teddy cradled her in his arms, pushing back into her, mimicking her every

movement. The heat was rising in the car as she reached down his

chest, caressing his muscular body, and giving into all of her emotions.

Teddy started kissing her neck, putting his hands through her hair, and

moving them sweetly down her back; completely absorbed in the

moment, until Amelia stopped cradling her leg. Pain ran through her

body, as she tried to work through the cramping that was taking over

every part of her. She twisted in a way she shouldn't have in the heat

of the moment. The pain slowly subsided as Teddy stared at her

guessingly.

Amelia finally asked, "Teddy, can you please help me out of

the truck to stretch and stand up? I think it might help with the pain."

She panted slightly.

Teddy was over on the other side of the truck before she even

finished her sentence, guiding her out, looking at her worryingly. She

looked back at him, and they both burst out laughing and blushing.

"How crazy are we? Or am I, I should say!" she stammered,

looking at her feet, catching her breath. Teddy was standing next to her, acting like her rock keeping her safe. Amelia looked up and glanced around her, seeing a ravine with caution tape across the road. She looked horrified at Teddy as this suddenly triggered her into a flashback.

Blood dripping down her face, she looked over at her to see how she was, but she wasn't there. She called for Chloe, stuck in the driver's seat, airbag deployed, and her seat belt stuck. She started screaming, looking for her phone, begging for Chloe to answer. Through the fog, she could barely see what looked like a person laying 10 feet in front of the car, not moving. A man ran up to her window, banging, "Hey, are you okay?" but he seemed so far away. The car was mangled, they hit a tree, and she started to puke. The ambulance arrived, and people tried to pry open her door. She screamed, "Chloe, get Chloe, I can't find her." She held her pounding head in her hands, crying. She just knew something was wrong. She was frantically motioning for them to help her, why wasn't anyone rushing to help her? Then she looked over and saw a stretcher, thank god, but wait no, wrong direction. Pointing over to where she thought Chloe was laying, she looked up just as they placed a white sheet over her body. Gone, no it can't be, it should be me, no…. She yelled, "Save her, you're not

trying, SAVE HER!" In that last breath, she felt suddenly woozy and

looked over to a paramedic removing a needle from her arm. That was

the last thing she saw as it got suddenly darker around her.

Teddy was shaking her saying, "Amelia, Amelia, are you okay?
I didn't realize this was where your accident was; I just pulled over
quickly because you were screaming."

She snapped out of the moment and looked at him so pale and
breathing heavily. "I, I, I'm okay. I'm tired. Can we go home?"

Teddy helped her into the truck with worry all over his face.
They drove home in silence, she felt exhausted and embarrassed.
Thinking to herself about the flashback, she hadn't had a flashback in
so long. It has been a couple of years since the last one; she couldn't
believe how weak she was, how vulnerable. *What is happening to me?*
I need Tune, I just want to hold Tune. Or maybe have Teddy hold me,
as she thought back to their passionate entanglement earlier.

When they arrived back at the vineyard, Teddy carried her back
inside. She could get use to this she thought. Amelia just felt at home

when she was in his arms, she had never experienced the feeling before, but she knew she wanted to be with him. Teddy brought her a pair of his pajamas and left her in the bathroom to get ready for bed. It was early for bed, but these days she couldn't get enough sleep and was always tired. It frustrated her, how long it took her to do such a simple task, as to change and go to the bathroom, but finally, she called for Teddy. He came in, scooped her up and brought her to his room.

Laying her in bed, he said, "Tomorrow, I will fix up the guest house for you, I will sleep in the living room tonight."

Amelia asked, "Teddy, would you mind staying with me, I just don't want to be alone tonight. Plus, I might need something, and I can't move." She blushed and looked at the sheets.

Teddy agreed, picking up her chin to meet his eyes. "I'd never let anything happen to you, yes I'll stay. I can set up an air mattress on the floor."

Amelia stared at him. "Build a barrier with Sapphire and Tune and sleep in the bed. It'll be fine. You're not sleeping on the floor! Or

you can cuddle with me, like you did when we were in the hospital."
She could feel her skin getting blotchy.

Teddy sheepishly smiled and agreed, "I'll be in later. I have
some things to tend to."

Tucking her in and leaving her with her medicine, he bid her
goodnight. Amelia laid there, rubbing Tune's belly, kissing his ears as
she thought about the craziness of the last two weeks. Amelia didn't
know if it was exhaustion or feeling completely content in the
moment, but either way she drifted off into a peaceful sleep.

Chapter 6

Amelia awoke early the next morning, but Teddy was already getting up and buttoning his shirt when she rolled over to look for Tune. Tune was at Teddy's feet wagging his tail waiting for some attention. Amelia never saw Tune interact this way with Elliot. *If Tune liked him, that had to be a good sign*, she thought to herself smiling.

She said, "Good morning, what did you do to Tune for him to love you so much? He's never like this with anyone but me," she smirked as she tried to tame her hair.

Teddy laughed. "Must be my southern charm and hospitality!"

She found herself smiling and couldn't believe how natural things felt with Teddy. It was like she has known him her whole life, and that scared her. Amelia thought back to her relationship with

Elliot, she wouldn't even let him stay over for the first six months, never mind sleep in the same bed together.

She sheepishly asked, "Can you take me to the bathroom? Maybe you can get me a walker so that I can move a little on my own and not have to constantly bother you."

Teddy looked at her. "Amelia, you have therapy tomorrow, and we can ask then, okay? I don't want you to risk injuring your leg or arm till the doctor says it is okay."

She knew he was right, but it made her upset, she hated being so dependent on someone else. After breakfast, Teddy brought her out to the barn to hang out in the den. As he carried her out, she was able to see the vineyard for the first time; she thought it was breathtaking.

"Do you do tasting and everything here?" Amelia asked.

Teddy said, "Oh, yes we do, it's a little slow right now, but the weekends are pretty busy. I'll take you over later today and give you a tour if you'd like."

Amelia shook her head yes, as she was so intrigued by it all. Teddy set her down on a rocking chair with an ottoman to prop her leg up, a cup of coffee, and a book.

"I'll see you in a few hours." Teddy set off for town.

Amelia sat there looking out of the window and started thinking back about her first time drinking wine. She had never really dabbled in wine or alcohol for that matter until a few years ago, but just enough to know what she liked and didn't like. Because of her past, she never lost control with her drinking. All through college, she ran a taxi service for campus students, to ensure they got home safely for free. It was the least she could do. She called it *Wheels for Chloe*, and it was a way for Amelia to try to right her wrongs for what she did. Although nothing would ever be enough for taking her life; it helped her to give back. Thinking of these thoughts sent her into another flashback.

She was arrested at the hospital and handcuffed to the bed like a criminal. Amelia woke up, realizing she was cuffed to the bed rails, panic set in with the realization that it wasn't a nightmare, and Chloe was really gone. She would never forgot the look on her mother's face, and the white sheet spread over Chloe; the image burned into her brain permanently. Once she was released from the hospital for her injuries, she was tried in a court and sentenced to four years in a juvenile delinquent facility for intoxicated manslaughter. Amelia was 16 at the time, and the court tried her as a minor. At the juvenile correctional facility, she went to therapy weekly after attempting to take her own life after an incident with a group of other young adults there. She couldn't bear with the fact that she lived and Chloe died; it was unfair, and she couldn't understand why! The constant pain from her injuries, grief, and guilt she felt for drinking and driving under the influence was overwhelming. The fact that her actions directly resulted in killing her brother's girlfriend and her best friend Chloe never left her. She eventually came to terms with what she did, enough to not want to kill herself. She used this experience to help others; she was met to live through this to educate others. Through her four years at Carbone Hall in Massachusetts, she would go to high schools and colleges giving presentations about her experience. She had branded herself Amelia: the Drunk Driver or Amelia: the Drunk Killer when *she presented, and this usually left her in tears on stage. Amelia would*

get stacks of letters from students that said, "You coming and telling

your story, has made me make better decisions. #justiceforchloe

#antidrunkdriving" Amelia had made this her trademark when

presenting to help spread her message. Once she was out and on a

probation period, Amelia was able to find a job. Her crime was wiped

from her record because she was a minor, and unless she got in trouble

again with the law, it would stay hidden. She was able to get her

license, but she had to have a breathalyzer installed for a year. Amelia

was so embarrassed, but never complained because she felt her

punishments weren't enough for what she did to Chloe and her family.

Chloe's parents sued her mother, Drew didn't speak to her again for

five years, and left town as soon as she was arraigned in court.

Amelia lost all her friends and her best friend that night, her mother

was the only person to visit and write to her.

Amelia was rubbing her fingers absentmindedly along her

scars, silent tears rolling down her face, while she thought back to this

time in her life. The burns and cutting scars marked her arms, Amelia

wanted to cover them in tattoos but never could bring herself to do it.

She never felt she deserved to forget this part of her past or to cover it up any more than it already was. Now with the new accident, her arms were marked up even more, her life was like a map on her body, and every scar had a story that made Amelia who she was today.

Tune and Sapphire rarely left her side all morning. Sapphire was a beautiful tan and white Pit bull mix, with beautiful bridling on her paws, which Teddy got as a puppy. As Amelia was changing her dressings and looking at the snake bite, she guessed she was about seven years old. She had slowly shuffled herself to the ground to treat Sapphire, but couldn't get back up. Now she was stuck on the ground until Teddy returned. The wounds were healing nicely, Sapphire was still favoring her other leg, but getting better each day. She didn't mind being down there, but couldn't stay there for too long. She was yelling, "Hello, anyone?" every time she heard a noise, until finally, someone heard her.

A young women came rushing in. "Oh my gosh, are you okay?" Rushing to her aid to help Amelia back in the chair, the woman introduced herself. "Hi, we haven't met, I'm Ella Pevotella, are you Tune's mom?"

Amelia looked up, "Hi Ella, yes, I'm Amelia, are you Teddy's sister?" Ella sat across from her on the couch.

"Yes, I'm his younger sister, and Sophia is our older sister and she's married, and lives up the road on the far side of the vineyard with her husband, Todd Wallock.

Amelia was looking at her, she felt like she was getting sucked in; her voice was so soothing and quiet. She was a prettier version of Teddy, but looked just like him. She was shorter with dirty blonde hair and perfect olive skin and piercing green eyes.

Ella started rambling, "I just broke up with this guy, Josh. I really liked him, but I found out he was cheating on me and he wasn't very nice to be either. I don't even know why I'm still thinking about him, I can't seem to help myself. I get so upset and angry at the same time because he still affects me so much. Do you know what I mean?" As she sighed heavily, drawing in breathe.

Ella was talking to Amelia about her guy troubles, and Amelia found herself easily talking about Elliot to her. This surprised Amelia, because she had never felt inclined to share stories about her life before.

"I do actually. Elliot was the only guy I was with in college; we were together for four years. He was abusive though, he had quite the temper and would yell, call me names, and break things when we fought. I was always very closed off with him, never could get that book romance, and love where I felt so comfortable, that I was compelled to share my deepest thoughts. It was one of our biggest issues, he would say how he never knew anything about me, and how even our intimacy was closed off. I was so heartbroken when he left me, and I still struggle with it; I feel like it was my fault it didn't work out. It's been about 7 months since he left me, and it still hurts. I could understand how you feel."

Ella was an amazing listener, and when Amelia finished, she said, "Amelia, I would say sorry, but it sounds like him leaving was a blessing to you. I always feel that the vibrations that another person gives off to you when you're together and especially intimate, sets the tone for how open the communication will be between the two people. If you don't feel safe, then you're naturally going to be closed off.

Instead of Elliot trying to get to know you, and be interested in your past, present and future; he was more concerned about his own feelings. You need a giver, not a taker, Amelia."

Amelia looked at her with her mouth wide open. "Ella, no one has ever been that real to me before, matter of fact, I never can talk about it much either. Thank you, I needed to hear this, but it's still hard to swallow. If you don't mind me saying, maybe you should take your own advice? Because of my past, I never let anyone in too deep to protect them I use to think, but now I realize it was to protect myself more than anything. I don't ever want to hurt anyone again…" Amelia's voice started to crack and the next thing she knew she was crying.

Ella hopped up and came over to hug her and Amelia felt herself give in to the connection Ella was giving her. She could smell brown sugar and vanilla extract on her as she was struggling to take a deep breath.

After a minute or so Ella stood up and started walking to the door looking back. "I know exactly what we need, I'll be right back Amelia, don't move!" she giggled and walked out of the barn.

Ella came back with Rhoda, carrying wine, cheese board, three glasses, and a little folding table. "Sounds like a solid girls day is in order, so I brought all the necessities to you!"

Amelia was surprised. "Oh wow Ella, you don't have to do this. I know you probably have so many other things to do today."

Ella waved her off, "Definitely don't, this is the best therapy, and I brought some lavender to help relax us! I invited Rhoda to join us because she's been going through a rough time too."

Amelia looked over, "Thank you, this looks lovely, what are we drinking?

Rhoda chimed in, "This is the best red blend you'll ever have, and it is called *Sapphire's Desire*, after Teddy's dog."

Rhoda walked over to see the snake and started asking questions about her schooling and about reptiles. Amelia was pleased to see someone else interested. She quickly told them her dream to open her own clinic and how she just wanted to help animals live a better life. Rhoda was so interested that she inquired about helping her out if she stayed in Indiana. Together they decided to name the mother snake Esmeralda. And from that moment on they Rhoda and Amelia had a bond.

The next thing, they were all laughing and crying. Amelia thought to herself, *this must be what it's like to have friends*. This went on for a couple of hours until Teddy came home with a burnt cardboard box.

Teddy walked in like it was nothing new. "Hello ladies! Amelia, I got some things for you in town." He brushed her shoulder as he walked by. "I see Ella's helping manage your pain with wine. I do think you need to take your pain medications soon though."

Amelia blushed, "With dinner okay, I don't want to mix wine and my medications, I'm okay right now.

Teddy nodded and headed out calling back, "I'm going to start dinner, you ladies staying?"

Both of Ella and Rhoda looked at Amelia for guidance until Amelia yelled, "Yes they are!"

They all giggled and picked up the conversation from where they left off. Amelia couldn't remember a better day since she got Tune. Her heart felt so full, and she found herself feeling happy and blessed to have crashed in Indiana. All while hoping it wasn't too good to be true, as she took a sip of wine.

Chapter 7

The next day, Amelia woke up and started going through the cardboard box Teddy had put next to the nightstand. Almost everything was ruined except for the necklace and one picture of her mom, her dad, Drew and herself when they were babies. Amelia put the necklace on immediately and planned to never take it off again. She felt better as soon as the necklace lay on her chest. As Teddy walked by, he said, "That's beautiful Amelia." This made Amelia so happy. "It was my grandmothers before it was my mom's. It's the one piece I have left."

The picture was burnt all along the edges, so that just their faces could be seen and there was a dark film over them, but she was happy to have at least one picture. It overwhelmed her with emotion. Not one person from this photo was active in her life or alive. That saddened her, especially having spent yesterday with Ella. She felt

Teddy was so lucky to have a family that loved him. Amelia only ever knew what a broken family was, and she saw first-hand how that broke her mother down when she was alive. Abandonment was a feeling that Amelia knew all too well. Maybe this was why she was always so closed off, she didn't want to risk breaking down her wall to get hurt again. Lately, that wall was starting to crumble, crack, and become weak. She was overwhelmed by her acceptance and care here, that she didn't exactly know how to handle it. What exactly was her relationship with Teddy? They only kissed those few times, but Amelia found herself thinking of it often and dreaming of a life with Teddy. Would she ever be able to share her past with him? Would he reject her, find her repulsive after all that they've been through?

The next morning, they woke up, and both got ready to go to therapy. Amelia was nervous, she didn't know what to expect.

Teddy seemed to be reading her mind. "Amelia, it's going to be okay, I'll be there for whatever you want me to be there for. I don't want to invade your space, so just let me know."

Sweet, Amelia thought to herself, but hated to feel so needy, she responded, "Let me see how it goes, I never seem to know what I want these days, so can we just take it as it comes?"

Teddy smiled and nodded, then left to go pull the truck around. It was a beautiful sunny morning in Indiana, about 60 degrees out, with a light breeze. She could smell the wine grapes mixed with the scent of nature.

He carried her out and she smiled and thanked him. "Hopefully that will be the last time you have to carry me, and I can start using a walker today!"

"I don't mind, I do hope to hear good news for you today," Teddy said. Amelia knew he was right to be cautious.

It was a thirty minute drive to therapy, but she found herself immersed in the scenery and the sun hitting her face.

She looked over and found Teddy smirking at her. "What?" Amelia said.

Teddy looked over and smiled. "You look cute when you sing and move to the music while enjoying the view, and so am I."

Amelia blushed; she hadn't even realized she was doing it. "I didn't even realize, sorry!" Amelia said giggling.

He pulled up to the rehab center, and a man came out with a wheelchair and helped Amelia have a seat.

Teddy closed the door. "I'll see you inside," he smiled to her as the facility greeter wheeled her inside.

Amelia met with her therapist, Colin. He brought her in and removed her cast on her arm. Colin took an X-ray and came out to give her the news.

"Amelia, I'm going to switch you to a soft cast for your arm, I'm going to remove the stitches, and we will test your motor function since the nerve surgery. The fracture has healed well in the last few weeks, you will start therapy to see your function capabilities," said Colin.

Amelia nodded; it felt so weird to have air hit her arm after all this time. Nevertheless, the progress made her happy. After he removed the stitches, he moved her hand, wrist, and arm to see the range of motion. Then he gave her a stress ball to hold and had her try to squeeze it, then grab on to a bike handle, and held it out. After he did some exercises with her, he gave her a sheet with some exercises to do at home 3 times a day till she came back in two days.

Amelia asked, "Can I get a walker to help me get around at home?"

Colin said, "No, not yet, I don't want you to put that much pressure on your arm. I can give you a wheelchair to use for the next few weeks."

Amelia sighed, she understood, but it was frustrating, "Okay, I understand, how much longer until I can try walking again?"

Colin looked at her encouragingly. "Amelia, let us do this one step at a time, if we move too fast, we can do more damage than good. The cast can't even be removed for four weeks. Then we can assess your progress after we take a new X-ray. Hang in there, it'll be okay."

Amelia came back out to the truck, and Teddy packed the wheelchair and helped Amelia in. She was so quiet most of the ride home, hiding her face from Teddy. He reached over and grabbed her hand and squeezed it softly. She looked over at him and responded bringing a smile to her face.

Teddy stopped at a red light and locked eyes with her. "I know it wasn't what you wanted to hear, progress is still better than bad news. We can get through this, we will do your exercises, and it will come." He turned back to the road and continued driving.

Amelia gave a weak smile. "Thank you for helping me and caring for me, I'm just not always great at holding back when I'm upset, all my plans are on hold, I need clothes, a car, and I don't even know how I'll afford a new one." She was venting and dumped all her worries before she could stop herself. "Sorry."

He smiled. "It's okay, I'm sure both my sisters have clothes you can have. When we get back, how about I take you on a tour of the vineyard to cheer you up?"

Amelia squeezed his hand encouragingly and smiled. "I think I'd like that."

As Teddy pulled into the vineyard she saw the sign *Pevotella Vineyard*. She noticed it needed a touch-up job, and also thought to herself that she could see it saying Veterinary Hospital underneath. She couldn't believe herself, but she had this uncanny connection to Teddy that made her feel like home or her idea of home because she never felt she had that feeling before.

Teddy stopped after they rounded the corner, put the car in park, and moved towards Amelia gently turning her chin towards him to kiss her. The butterflies in her stomach consumed her as she fell into a blissful state. He finally pulled back. "I have been dying to do that since you were singing and dancing earlier." Kissing her forehead, he slid back over to the driver's seat; Amelia reached over caressing his arm as they drove up to the house. He came around and picked her up, she started running her hand up and down his neck and through his hair, Teddy let out a small groan. Amelia, aroused, started drifting off thinking about them intimately together. He placed her on the couch in the barn and went to close the door. As he was walking back, she watched him, loving everything that she was seeing. He was so sexy and intriguing. Amelia couldn't believe he was single and interested in her.

Teddy sat down next to her, both eager to start kissing again, becoming familiar with each other, falling into a space where everything else seemed to melt away. Amelia unbuttoned his shirt and was running her hands down his chest and around his back taking in all of his body. He started groaning in her ear and kissing down her neck tracing his finger along her collar bone causing Amelia to moan out loud giving in to all of him. Teddy looked down at her as if taking in her beauty, and she reached up to cup her hands around his neck to pull him close, intertwined, in complete bliss.

After a while, Teddy sat up tucking her hair behind her ear, "Tell me something about the real Amelia? I want to know everything."

Amelia was shocked. She stammered, "You wouldn't like her. I don't want to ruin a good moment. I'd rather hear about you!"

Teddy was taken aback by this. "What could you possibly say to make me not like you? You're amazing and caring and-"

"NO I'm not…. stop saying things you don't know anything about!" Amelia stammered.

Teddy appalled, "Amelia, why are you so upset, I just want to get to know you. I don't understand why you are being so hard on yourself?"

Amelia, wishing she could walk away, turned to him, "Oh, I don't know, maybe- Death, bad decisions, jail... I could go on."

Teddy was looking at her, trying to gauge her emotions. "Amelia, if you're in trouble, I can help. Jail? What happen?"

Amelia felt herself losing control of her emotions. "Are you always Mr. Nice— always saying the right thing? Why are you still single then?" she snapped.

Teddy stood up, raising his voice with frustration. "After everything you just said, you're worried about why I'm single? Really Amelia. You could just ask nicely, and I would have told you. Also, aren't you around the same age, so I could say the same to you." He seemed in complete disbelief on how this turned out.

Amelia was appalled by this. "I killed someone that's why, okay! No one wants someone like me. I actually never let anyone get this close because of this. You can go now. You don't have to stare."

Teddy stormed off yelling, "Always on your terms, fine, you want to be alone, you stubborn woman."

Amelia broke down in tears, pissed off she let something like that out. *I can't believe I did that. What is wrong with me? Who am I?*

Before she could work through her thoughts, Teddy came storming back. "You need your medications and do you need anything before I leave you alone as requested."

She looked up, embarrassed. "I need to go to the bathroom, actually if you don't mind and I'm hungry, I need to eat before I can take my medication." Heat flushed her cheeks.

He swooped her up and brought her to the bathroom and back. "I'll be back with some food and your medications," he said, walking away before she had a chance to say anything else.

Ugh, this is bad. Why did I do something like this knowing I can't go anywhere for at least four weeks and have no car! She started banging her head against her fist when she was interrupted by an unfamiliar voice.

"Are you okay miss?"

Amelia shot her head up. An older man was standing at the door.

"Hi, sorry you had to witness that, not one of my better moments. I'm Amelia, Tune is my dog and Teddy has been nice enough to allow me to stay here while I'm healing from my accident."

He stepped forward and came to sit down next to her with his hand out. "I'm Theodore Pevotella Sr., Teddy's dad, but you can call me Ted. I started this vineyard with my late wife 35 years ago. Welcome. Teddy told us all about you."

The two got acquainted and starting talking about wine. He was such a nice man. Amelia guessed he was in his 70's. She was glad for the distraction and was also sucked into the conversation about wine.

He was giving the history of the vineyard when Amelia abruptly cut in. "What made you guys want to open a vineyard and weren't you worried about not being successful?"

Ted looked inquisitively at Amelia, "Let me ask you, Amelia, what career path have you set yourself on?'

Immediately Amelia knew where this was going but answered anyways. "I was on my way to California to start over. I want to open my own Veterinary Hospital called *Wags to Whimpers*."

Ted listened and then spoke softly. "And aren't you worried you won't make it, what made you decide to open your own? Why not become a partner somewhere or just work at another vet hospital."

Amelia chuckled. "I get it. I might fail, I might not, can't tell the future, but what I can tell you is that I'm determined to make a better life for myself."

Ted smiled. "That is exactly what my wife and I wanted for our family. To create a safe haven, and show our children what hard work and dedication does. If you don't mind me asking, what are you running away from? California is pretty far away."

Amelia frowned. "Cat's out of the bag with Teddy now anyway, I don't know if anyone will understand, but it's done now, and I can't take it back."

Ted stared intently at her, "I promise to try to understand and help you if you want me to."

Amelia weakly smiled. "Thank you, I don't know how to help myself anymore. When I was 16 years old, I killed my best friend Chloe in a car accident. I was driving, and I was drunk. She was ejected on impact and died on the scene. I was tried as a minor and spent four years in juvenile prison. I haven't had a relationship with my brother, Drew, since the accident. Chloe was also his girlfriend at the time. He has never forgiven me, and we barely speak." She abruptly covered her mouth, shocked at how honest it was.

Ted placed a hand on her shoulder and lightly squeezed it. "You were just a teenager Amelia. Should you have known better, yes, but you paid your time. You need to try and let go of your guilt, your remorse, and try to use those feelings to expel them wisely upon others. Easily said than done, I'm sure, but look at what you've accomplished. Create your roots and grow into the beautiful person you are, and let that shine through. You are, what, 30 now? It's been almost 15 years since this happened; it's time."

Amelia silently cried, listening intently to Ted. Feeling this sense of relief for finally talking about her past, the burden she felt, and how she didn't feel she should be happy. "I don't deserve to feel better, I ended a life, and I ruined a family. I feel like I should always feel the pain I feel. The looks people back home would give me, the disgrace I became in town, I always have been so alone."

Ted got up. "I will be right back, give me one minute." Amelia wished she could run away, but the fact that she was forced to stay put didn't bother her as much as she thought it would. Moments later Ted returned with a file in his hand. This piqued Amelia's interest, what could he be about to share with her? Ted handed her the envelope. "Read this, I will be back soon," and he walked out to the barn.

Amelia waited till she was alone and then hesitated. She felt weird opening it. It was so old, smelt musky, and had a faded shape of a rectangle around it like a book had been sitting on it for a long time. She pushed the metal tabs up and flipped the envelope open. At first glance, there were some newspaper articles and a photo. Amelia immediately went for this small, square, black, and white photo. On the back it said, "Ted, Tim, and John 1963." The three boys looked like they were 12-14 years old. She stared at the photo for a while before she reached back in the envelope. The newspaper article was titled:

"Teen dies while racing tractors with friends." The article went on to read about how Ted, Tim, and John decided to race on Willmaker's Farm at dusk on July 15, 1963. Tim Willmaker was racing on the family farm tractor with his friends when the tractor hit a rock causing Tim to lose control of the tractor, slamming on the breaks. The jerk of the tractor made Tim fall off and was pronounced dead at the scene of the accident. Tim was 12 years old, and John and Ted were 13 year-old friends of Tim. Both of the boys were given community service and weren't able to get their driver's license until they were 18 according to Indiana judge that resided that day in court.

Amelia was crying and reached back into the envelope, to find another newspaper clipping of the obituary for Tim, and one about the Willmaker's farm sold after a freak accident killed the son.

Ted came back in with a bottle of white wine and two glasses and some cheese. She chuckled darkly. "Is this what your family does every time there's an issue?"

Ted laughed, "Why yes, this is one of the only ways we know how to talk through hard times." He placed the glasses down and poured her a glass. "This is a wine I named in memory of Tim, it's called "*Tres Blanco*."

Amelia smiled weakly, the bottle had the black and white photo on it, with in memory of Tim on the bottom.

Ted handed her the glass, "It took me a long time to work through this so-called freak accident that was my fault. It was my idea to race tractors, I was a bully and pressured my best friend to do this, and it ended up costing him his life. I can still hear his scream before he died, I still have nightmares, and I still battle with my happiness. His dad and mom moved and sold their farm, they eventually had a baby girl, but the trauma I caused Tim's family is unimaginable to most. You understand, because you feel the same way I still feel, but I had to move forward, and make the best of my life for Tim. It would be even worse if I wasted my life and took his. You should do the same, make Chloe look down on you and be proud. She would never want you to be miserable and unhappy, she would want you to live your best life and enjoy it."

Amelia listened while sipping her wine thoughtfully, then finally broke her silence. "How long did it take you?"

Ted sighed, "A while, the disappointment and the negativity I brought on my family was just as hard, but they stood by me and made sure I made it as right as I could. I did the difficult things, and I even teach Tractor Safety to tell my story, hoping it helps make a difference. It wasn't till I met Miranda that I was able to be fully happy, she helped me cope in ways, I didn't know how to. She saved me, she had a passion for wine and always wanted to start her own vineyard, and with that being so, that was what my goals became. I loved her so much and felt so blessed to be given the chance to experience love. Miranda loved me for me and not my past; at first, I felt I didn't deserve her. How could I get so lucky? In time, I learned what I'm trying to convey to you today." Ted pulled out his wallet, and tucked under for a picture of Miranda was a very old piece of paper, unfolded and folded so many times, it was barely holding on; in cursive handwriting it read

"The Edge- There is no honest way to explain it because the only people who really know where it is are the ones who have gone over.
- Hunter S. Thompson."

Its edges were torn, and the ink was so faded, Amelia barely could make it out. As she started reading it out loud, Ted chimed in and finished it for her, all the while staring blankly out towards the barn door. "I've read that every day for a year, and use to pull it out when times got tough. Now I just repeat it now and then when I need it." He folded it back up and handed it to Amelia. "I want you to have this as a reminder that you aren't alone, you are strong, and you will overcome this battle, to live a beautiful life."

Amelia hugged Ted, crying. "I've never had a male figure in my life to talk to like this. My dad left us when I was 2 and Drew was 7. I haven't seen him or spoken to him since before I was arrested. I don't even know how to thank you for taking time to talk to a stranger and share Tim's story with me. I will cherish this moment forever." She hugged the folded up note to her chest. "I hope Teddy will understand, he was so angry and stormed out. I understand why Teddy is who he is; you're an amazing father and raised him well. He literally saved

Tune and I and hasn't left my side since. I don't know how I got so lucky, I don't deserve all that he's done already." She took a deep breath, sipped her wine and ate some cheese, trying to steady her breathing. Then looked over to Ted and there were tears in his eyes. "I'm so sorry, what did I say? This is why I'm better alone, I don't want to hurt anyone……"

Ted reached over and embraced her, "Shhhhhhh, it is okay, take a deep breath. It is therapeutic for me as well to share my story and see the impact. I'm just as touched by this interaction as you are. You need to give yourself more credit, you have a beautiful soul."

Amelia cried and melted into his embrace, thinking of how this was what she always wanted from Jeremy and never got.

She finally calmed down enough to sit back, wiping her tears as Ted handed her a napkin. "Thank you, so much Ted. Ella and Sophie are very lucky to have you."

Ted went to say something when the barn door opened and Teddy walked in holding a tray of food. "Hey dad, when did you get back, I see you've met Amelia."

Ted stood up and picked up the envelope. "Yes, we just had a lovely chat, she's a real catch son. Come see me later at the house, so I can catch you up on my business trip." Ted walked out waving back at Amelia, "See you soon, my dear."

Amelia waved back and smiled and watched Teddy close the door and walk towards her. "Hi, I brought you an array of options because I didn't know what you'd be in the mood for or liked. I realized as I was cooking that I don't know that much about you, so then I kind of got out of hand….." he trailed off staring at his feet.

They both suddenly said, "I'm sorry," followed with laughter.

Amelia looked up at Teddy. "Join me?"

Teddy was relieved, "I'd love to join you." He sat down and pulled everything closer, poured a glass of wine in Ted's empty glass and raised it to Amelia, "Cheers" they clinked glasses and took sips staring at each other intently. "Look, Amelia, I didn't mean to lose my temper and yell. I'm really sorry, you can be quite frustrating. I feel like I never know what is going to happen with us from moment to moment. I'm still trying to navigate all this."

Amelia smiled. "Teddy, I should be the one to apologize, you asked me a harmless question, and I lost my mind and freaked out. You couldn't have guessed that. I'm a nutcase lately, and I'm so sorry and very appreciative of your patience. I never have let anyone in this deep before and following my trauma, I just never expected to wake up to you. It's like I'm dreaming and it's just too good to be true. I don't deserve you."

Teddy was staring at her like she was the only woman in the world. Amelia's heart was pounding out of her chest, and she yearned to feel his touch and the warmth of his body against hers. *Is this what love is? Is this real?* His eyes, piercing hazel green color, with little specks of yellow in them. His jawline was so strong, and she was starting to realize that he clenches when he's nervous. He was perfect from head to toe.

Then she realized he was saying, "Hey where'd you run off to in that mind of yours? Have you heard anything I've just said?"

Amelia blushed, "I'm so sorry, this meal looks delicious, and I'm famished. Shall we enjoy?"

Teddy smiled. "Yes we have all the time in the world to get to know each other, let us just sit and appreciate one another's company."

They ate and laughed till they cried, all Amelia could think to herself was, *I could do this with him forever. Could Teddy be my Miranda?* This went on for hours until they fell asleep on each other's shoulders.

Chapter 8

Amelia woke up the next morning in Teddy's bed with a start as she heard Tune barking. "Tune, what's wrong buddy?"

All she heard was Ella saying, "Shhh... Tune, you're going to wake mommy, and she needs her rest!"

Amelia yelled back, "Too late!" laughing afterwards.

Ella came in, "Sorry Amelia, I tried to keep them quiet, but there's always a lot of traffic here on the weekend. Can I help you at all?"

Amelia smiled. "It is okay, can you bring my wheelchair over? I'll get dressed, and then we can have breakfast. I'm starving, and I need to medicate."

Ella wheeled it over. "Teddy made you breakfast and left you a note at the table," she said, smirking she walked away.

Amelia groaned in frustration. *Now what?* she thought. He was always up to something. She wheeled herself out to the kitchen after she got ready, and saw a vase of sunflowers and a note leaning up against it.

Amelia -

'We do not believe in ourselves until someone reveals that deep inside us something is valuable, worth listening to, worthy of our trust, sacred to our touch. Once we believe in ourselves, we can risk curiosity, wonder, spontaneous delight or any experience that reveals the human spirit.'

-E. E. Cummings

xoxo Teddy

She read it and smiled. Tears welling up in her eyes, she grabbed her coffee and melted away. The sunflowers were so vibrant and beautiful; she reread the quote at least 20 times while she ate her breakfast of fresh berries, an omelet with spinach, tomato, goat cheese, and onion, and some wheat toast. It was delicious, and she loved how much color he cooked with. Or maybe it was the amazing mood she was in, she couldn't tell and didn't care. She couldn't remember a happiness like this; she was feeling lighter than she did in years. It sparked her to want to write a thank you note to Ted. As she was thinking about everything; the door opened, and Ella came in beaming.

"Are you all set? I came to get you out to the vineyard! Come on." Ella said.

Next thing she knew, Amelia was being wheeled out to the driveway and down to her car. Ella helped her in and skipped back to the driver's side. Amelia was wide-eyed looking at her like she was crazy. She turned the car on, she drove a baby blue Volkswagen beetle car, and it fit her personality perfectly.

"Ella, you are so excited, what's going on?" Amelia as looking over at her smirking and trying not to laugh as Ella was dancing to the country music that was on. Luke Combs' "Beautiful Crazy" was playing.

"He's my favorite, sorry!" Ella beamed at her. "It's the weekend, and it is gorgeous out there, what's there not to be excited about?"

Amelia smiled. "True, I'm in a pretty great mood myself today! So where are we headed?"

Ella laughed in a devious way, "Can't tell you! It's a surprise!"

Amelia gasped in a fake surprise way, and then they both started laughing as Ella continued to drive towards Amelia's next adventure in Indiana.

Ella was driving on a dirt road on the Pevotella Farm for a good 10 minutes before Amelia finally asked, "Where do you live Ella? Do you live on the farm too?"

She looked over at Amelia. "Yes, we all do, our property is quite large, so it doesn't honestly ever feel like it. I live probably five minutes from Teddy's house."

"Oh wow, I didn't realize the property was that big, how many acres is it?" Amelia questioned.

Ella giggled, "Um, not that great at math, don't pay attention too much to those details. I have no idea, which sounds silly now that you asked."

They drove singing along to country songs, windows down a little, enjoying the sweet air of summer coming. The birds were chirping too. *It's so beautiful here*, Amelia thought to herself.

Ella pulled up to a beautiful tasting room, huge wrap around porch with tables, chairs, rocking chairs, and a huge deck off the back. "This is beautiful!" Amelia exclaimed.

Ella parked the car, got Amelia's wheelchair, and helped her out of the car. "Let's head in, you're going to love it."

As they went inside, Amelia was underwhelmed with how quiet it was. Back in Massachusetts, a place like this would be wall to wall with people. Amelia looked back at Ella. "Is this considered to be busy for you? Or is this a slower pace for the winery?"

Ella put her head down and whispered, "Don't say anything, but we have been struggling the last few years, just can't seem to get the same crowds anymore. About a year after my mom passed away, the winery has been struggling financially. We've been barely scraping by."

Amelia was shocked, "I'm so sorry, but I don't understand. The wine I've tasted is divine, I don't understand why?" She was thinking in her head, *I've got to do something*. Especially, with her marketing background in school, she could definitely help if they'd let her.

"Amelia, I'd like to introduce you to Sophia," Ella said as a beautiful woman with red hair, brown eyes, and a tad darker skin than Ella and Teddy appeared. She was about 6 feet tall, Amelia thought to herself. *Quite the gene pool, damn!*

"Hi Sophia, it's so nice to finally meet you!" Amelia said extending her hand which was completely ignored as she was overwhelmed with an embrace from Sophia.

"Amelia, we are so happy to have you are here and to finally meet you as well. I've heard so much about you, well from everyone it seems. How are you feeling? I'm so happy you're okay, and we just love Tune" Sophia said trying to catch her breath. She was so excited and friendly just like Ella.

"Speaking of Tune, do you know where he is?" Amelia asked.

Sophia and Ella giggled and answered simultaneously, "With Sapphire!" They pushed her wheelchair to the back where they were cuddling with their heads entangled on each other's back.

"They are always together; I think they're in love!" Ella said.

As soon as Tune heard Amelia, his tail started thumping against the floor, and he jumped up to greet her with kisses. Amelia missed his snuggles; she hugged up on him and then Sapphire wiggled in to get some love too. "Who's a beautiful girl, yes, you are! Okay, now who can sit for me, good boy and girl, paw!"

Ella came over with some treats and handed them to Amelia. "Here you go, Amelia for the babies."

Amelia beamed, "Ohhhh, look who has treats!" and they both started wagging their tales at her. It was so nice to see Tune with another dog. Amelia never thought he was lonely, but maybe he needed a companion too. She watched as they played with a toy and then went back to snuggling next to the fire in the wine tasting area.

Sophia and Ella sat down with Amelia at a table. It was set up so nice, the tables were wine barrels with wine corks as the tabletop covered with clear glass. Some shorter than others, then a beautiful cedar bar with high chairs going all the way down. It was the perfect set up. There was a slider door that led out to a beautiful garden, well what has potential to be, looks like it used to look elegant. *Maybe I can help build this place back up.* "Girls, do you ever have live music here?"

They both looked at her, intrigued. Sophia answered, "No, we haven't, I've been trying to convince my dad to let us try some new things. Can you tell me what that's like or what you're thinking?"

Amelia went on to explain, "You have music like karaoke, open mics, or hire a band to come sing for the guests. You can build up this garden for ambience. Maybe have some yard games for guests to play. You know, give people a reason to make this their Saturday destination. Maybe a food truck too? These are just some thoughts. What about social media for the vineyard?"

Ella was vigorously writing down everything she was saying. "This is great, Amelia! Sophia, what do you think? What if we put together a flyer and I know a band that would love to play here. They are like Bluegrass Country called "*Indiana Barrel Band*" It's three guys and a female singer. They are really good. I've heard them play a few times at the county fair!

Sophia listened before she spoke. "I love the enthusiasm, but how would we afford any of this? Let us face it, Ella, we are broke and barely afloat. That's why dad is so scared, we can't risk investing this type of money with no return."

Amelia was lost in her own thoughts. "Sorry to interrupt, but has anyone ever done their wedding here? Your property is a perfect location; I bet the sunsets are stunning."

Sophia jumped up, rambling about a bunch of details to the point where Ella screamed, "Sit down and talk slow, I can barely keep up!" Her handwriting was almost a scribble, she was writing so fast.

The next thing you know, the three of them had their heads together, coming up with all of these plans. This went on for a good hour or so before they were interrupted by a guest.

Ella jumped up to greet them, "I got this, guys, continue!"

Sophia and Amelia continued to talk about the land and the possibilities, then Sophia asked, "What do you have a degree in, what are your aspirations?"

Amelia started to tear up, "I… I… never have been surrounded by such nice people. No one back home has ever cared enough to ask me. I have a degree in marketing that I started when I was in juvie, and then when I got out, I went to school to become a veterinarian and finish my business degree as a minor."

Sophia looked wide-eyed at her. "Can I ask what you were in juvie for? I don't mean to pry, but you've piqued my interest, and I don't want to pressure you either."

Amelia said, "No, it's okay, it isn't an easy subject for me, but I'm trying to be better about it. I brought it up too, so it's natural for you to ask. When I was a teenager, I was at a party with my older best friend who also happened to be my brother's girlfriend at the time. Chloe and I were drinking, and Chloe was supposed to drive us home. I was trying to be cool and social. I was hanging with an older crowd; I thought I could handle it. Chloe drank too much and asked me to drive. I knew she couldn't and didn't think I couldn't; how wrong I was. I ended up crashing us into a tree and Chloe didn't have her seat belt on. She was ejected on impact and killed instantly. I was sentenced to four years at Carbone Hall; I've lived with regret every day. I don't understand why I survived, I tried to make the best from my poor decisions that night," Amelia trailed off into a whisper and then a momentary silence as she looked up at Sophia with tears running down her cheeks.

Sophia reached over to touch her hand. "Oh, Amelia, how awful, I can't imagine how you must feel. All I can say is, don't waste your life, guilt is an ugly thing that can consume and ruin a person's life. If you can't do it for you, do it for Chloe. I think it's wonderful that you got a career in something that gives you the ability to give back and help. That is something you should be so proud of, I bet Chloe would."

Amelia thanked Sophia for her kind words. "I'm going to try and not let my past take hold of my future. I'm going to try to be happy, and that's all I can do right now, I think."

Sophia nodded and then they started to look at Ella as she was giving the wine tasting.

Amelia took a sip of her wine and asked, "Your turn, what are your aspirations?"

Sophia smiled. "My husband, Todd, is a dentist and I'm a dental hygienist. I work about thirty minutes from here at the office that we own. On the weekends, I still like to work here at the winery. It's always been a passion of mine too."

"That's amazing. How is it working with your husband? I can understand you not wanting to let go of this place. It is home for you, I would think!" Amelia said while staring out to the beautiful landscape that surrounded them.

Sophia smirked. "It's challenging at times, but we are a great team. Somehow we always end up making it through the tough times stronger. We are truly lucky, I know a lot of our friends think it's weird that we work together and still want to be together at home." She chuckled and then sipped her wine. "But it works for us. And he's supportive of my family's business. Yes, we have disagreements, but who doesn't!"

"That is what I've been striving for in a relationship for most of my adult years. The kind of bond, reassurance, and support is amazing and rare. I think it's absolutely fantastic, I don't know who's luckier, Todd or you?" Amelia smiled raising her glass to Sophia.

Ella joined them, and they continued to enjoy each other's company until midday. Ella helped Amelia out to her car and drove her back home with Tune and Sapphire. Amelia starred out of the window reminiscing about her day, feeling full of love and exhaustion. She couldn't believe that just weeks ago, she felt so alone. So vulnerable for a new start in her life. Amelia beamed into the sunset thinking; she couldn't have picked a better place to crash.

Chapter 9

As Ella pulled into Teddy's driveway, Amelia became giddy with excitement. Teddy was standing outside on his front porch, next to a beautiful square table set with a canary, yellow table cloth, white linen napkins, 2 candlestick holders with lavender colored candles in them and white dishes set for two. He was dressed in a dark gray button-down shirt, dark blue jeans, gray suede cowboy hat and boots, holding a beautiful bouquet of gorgeous wildflowers in his hands, and a card. Amelia was at a loss for words. He looked stunning, and she tried to catch her breath before Ella noticed. Ella parked the car and hopped out, giving Teddy thumbs up as she rounded the front of her car, and she helped Amelia out and wheeled her to the front porch, where Teddy was patiently waiting.

She leaned down and whispered in her ear, "Enjoy Amelia!" She giggled with excitement as she waved back at them before driving away.

Teddy came down the stairs effortlessly, almost as he was floating towards her. As he reached her, he handed her the bouquet. "For you, you look beautiful today." A small color rose in his cheeks she noticed has he swooped Amelia up into his arms. "Hey, you come here often?" he joked, completely breaking the ice.

Amelia burst out laughing, turning to meet his smile. He leaned down to her and softly kissed her lips. Amelia would never admit this, but she was yearning for this all day, just to be in his arms. She couldn't put a finger on exactly what it was about it, but she felt safe, like no one could touch her, while in his presence.

"You think you're so slick, you smell amazing. I mean you look amazing. What is all of this? It looks beautiful." Amelia whispered to him as he carried her to her seat, slightly embarrassed that she'd commented on his scent.

Screw the food, I could stay in these arms forever. They seriously smell so good and look so handsome, she thought to herself. *No one has ever done anything like this for me before*. She was feeling full of life. As she looked over and smiled at Tune and Sapphire curled up together under the porch swing. Even they seemed so in love; this place is contagious. She shook her head and smiled, turning her attention back to Teddy.

"There you are, I lost you for a minute. How are you feeling today after therapy yesterday?" Teddy asked, while smiling at her across the table.

"Sorry, I was just thinking of how happy Tune is, how happy I've felt these last few days. I'm sore, but it is a good sore I think!" Amelia said, speaking so softly as if she didn't want to risk ruining the night with any of her outbursts.

Teddy seemed to perk up at her words. "I'm happy to hear this, my family seems to really adore you. I think Ella is a little attached." He chuckled.

She laughed. "You know, I think I'm getting attached, Sophia and Ella were amazing today. I never had a sister, it was wonderful today. Can you help me into my wheelchair, so I can run to the bathroom?" She always felt weird about being so needy but it was only temporary, she kept reminding herself.

"Of course." He grabbed her chair and helped her in. "I'm going to go grab our first course, I'll be right back." As he walked by her, he gently brushed her arm and headed to the kitchen.

Amelia's whole body felt heightened with goosebumps and butterflies from the little temptation Teddy gave her.

In the bathroom, she stared at herself trying to fix her hair as she touched up her face a bit. *Get a hold of yourself, Amelia— don't get too attached, this is temporary.* She kept telling herself in her head, *you don't want to hurt anyone or yourself.* The constant back and forth she felt lately about being closed off, was weighing her down. She didn't know what to do. Amelia composed herself and went back outside to wait for Teddy.

As she sat there and waited, all she could think about was how much she wanted more from him. This scared Amelia because she never was the type to be physically and emotionally tied to a person especially this quickly. Her mind was giving her whiplash, she was tempted by her attraction to abandon everything she's done for the past 12 years and to stay closed off.

Teddy came back out with two cups of soup. "Today, we have a delicious chicken soup with spinach, potato, and carrots." He placed it in front of her and poured her a glass of *Sunset Meadow Riesling*. He was trying to be so serious but couldn't and chuckled slightly.

"This smells delicious, and your winery has some exceptional wines. Today your sisters gave me a tasting menu, and I did one of them. They are all honestly good, do you guys ever enter in contests with them?" she asked as she started to eat her soup.

Teddy sighed. "I'm guessing the girls shared with you that we aren't doing well? We haven't done a lot of things since my mom died. It's been hard, but we obviously need to do something and very soon. We are just trying to get my dad on board."

"Yes, they did, but that's not why I'm saying this, the wine is really good. We talked about a lot of ideas today, and we don't have to do that now. Just surprised- generally seems to be the thought of the day. I'm so touched by everything you did today from my note and flowers this morning to this romantic evening." She could feel herself getting emotional.

Teddy and Amelia enjoyed their soup and talked about the vineyard for a while until Teddy got up to get the next course. He came back with a beautiful display of bread and cheese board and a delicious penne alla vodka dish. The food was incredible, when Amelia couldn't muster even one more bite, she sat back holding her hands on her stomach.

"Are you full? Are you sure you had enough? I have more!" Teddy said attempting to get up.

"If you bring me anything else, I'll burst! I'm so full, and it was perfect! Thank you!" She reached her hand over to pull his arm towards her.

He quickly came over to her and Amelia joked about how not being able to freely move was becoming an advantage. He picked her up and brought her over to the porch swing.

"Let me grab our drinks, the sun is about to set, it's stunning!" Teddy said as he retrieved their drinks and joined her on the swing.

He put his arm around her, and she quickly got comfortable leaning into his muscular, warm body. Teddy ran his fingers gracefully, flowing back and forth over her shoulder and down her arm. Amelia was tantalized by his touch silently begging for more, she was hoping it wouldn't end. She started to nuzzle her cheeks into his chest wishing she was warmer, but refused to mention it because she was thoroughly enjoying the moment. But Teddy seemed to catch on that she was chilly and got her a blanket to cover up. *He was like a dream, how could this be real life.* They sat there in each other's arms, watching the sunset behind the rolling hills in the distance. It was a beautiful evening, and Amelia couldn't have asked to be anywhere else.

As Amelia got colder, he decided to take her inside. He had the fireplace going with a set-up of pillows and blankets laid out in front of it. Teddy placed her down in front of the fire and covered her shoulders with the blanket.

"I'll be right back, I just have to bring in the food," Teddy said as he walked back outside.

Amelia warmed up nicely in front of the fire, awestruck with how much effort Teddy put into dinner tonight. He had twinkling lights set up to illuminate the room just right and compliment the roaring fire. The flames flickering in her eyes entranced her, she began to think about her day with the girls, and how happy she was when Teddy came to sit down behind her rubbing her shoulders. Amelia melted, she has never enjoyed someone else's touch more. She moaned lightly, Teddy brushed her hair to one side of her back, started kissing her bare shoulder, and slowly moved up her neck. Amelia fell back into his chest, as he continued up her chin to her lips. She was consumed with emotion as she lightly pushed him back. Staring at him, deeply looking into his eyes; she just knew, this is where she wanted to be forever.

"I think I'm in love with you, Teddy," she said it so softly that he barely heard her.

Teddy moved in front of her to graze her chin with his fingers, as he laced his fingers through her hair, and cupped it behind her ear. "I think I love you too, Amelia."

The passion that erupted from Amelia was like fireworks. The two of them couldn't keep their hands off each other passionately kissing and frantically removing each other's clothes, giving in to all of their temptations until Teddy rolled onto his back, both trying to catch their breath, softly laughing to one another. Laying there in silence, their heads facing each other, she was enjoying the moment, embracing the feelings that she always longed to have.

"Time for dessert!" Teddy said as they sat up. He wrapped the blanket around her body, gently grazing his teeth along her bare shoulder.

She giggled. "Can you take me to the bathroom please, I want to freshen up."

Teddy scooped her up and took her to the bathroom. He brought in her pajamas as well as she requested. Amelia hollered for Teddy when she was done. Teddy brought her back out and had dessert waiting for her.

"Boy do you think of everything!" Amelia grinned.

Teddy laughed. "Well, I made it, so don't get too excited. I'm not a great baker, but I made us some apple pie. Ella gave me a recipe, so fingers crossed, it's edible."

Amelia didn't really care for apples in general but didn't want to hurt his feelings. She ate it anyway. She didn't know if it was just because Teddy made it, but she didn't find it hard to eat it at all.

He looked at her cautiously. "Can I ask you about the other day? I would like to know more about what you meant."

Sighing, she said, "Yes, I can tell you. I just didn't want to ruin our evening with my poor life choices. I don't think you'll still think you love me after this conversation, but I don't want to hide from it anymore either. When I was 16, I left a high school party with my best friend. We were drunk, I thought I could drive, I ended up crashing, and she died."

"Are you serious Amelia? That's what you were referring to? I mean yes, true it's not a great story, but that doesn't define you. You messed up, you also were a teenager. Granted, I didn't have that happen to me, but I made poor life choices too that definitely could have ended that way or worse. I was just lucky. I'm so sorry that happened to you and your friend." Teddy tried to comfort her.

Amelia stammered, "Don't do that! Don't pretend like it doesn't change the way you view me!"

Teddy clenched his jaw, "Please tell me how you want me to respond? How can you sit there, and tell me how I feel?"

Amelia cried, as she had been a lot lately, it was really starting to piss her off. "I don't know. All I know is how I've been treated for the last 12 years of my life since this happened. You have no idea what I've been through, and I deserved it all. I ended a life and ruined two families!" she was taking deep breaths, trying to calm down.

"You are right, I have no idea, but that doesn't mean I don't want to. I'm not other people, I'm me. Please let me understand, let me love you." Teddy reached out to grab her hands. "Please, I may have not killed anyone, but I've been through things in my life that have changed me too," he said, tears running down his face.

Amelia immediately melted. "No, please don't do this, I don't want to hurt anyone else. Why are you crying? You shouldn't love someone like me, you deserve better than me. We barely know each other," she said as she wiped his tears away.

Teddy refused to look at her, "I can't handle another person walking away. Not a person I feel this deeply for. I know we haven't known each other for long, but at this point in your life, I feel like you know pretty quickly. Especially, when you can't stand to be away from them, your mind is always thinking of that person, and you find even when you're angry, you want to be with that person. It has to be love."

Amelia kissed Teddy, begging for his touch, his embrace, his love. He pulled back and she said, "Teddy, I want to love you and be what you need, but I'm scared. I don't know how to navigate this. I've been alone for years, and have become very good at it. It's my defense mechanism, so I don't get hurt, and I don't hurt anyone else. The only family I have is Drew, and we haven't had a relationship since I killed Chloe, his girlfriend at the time. My mom died five years ago, and my dad left when I was two. It has been Tune and me for five years. That is all the love I've known. Most of the time, I hate myself, my dad hates me, Drew hates me, and you probably will end up hating me too..." she trailed off looking out the window.

"My fiancé left me at the alter three years ago, and I haven't let anyone in either. Not until I came upon your car on fire. You are the first person I've fought for in three years. Between Stephanie abandoning me, and my mom passing away a few years ago. I've shut down since; it is just Sapphire and my family. Don't get me wrong, I love them all, and I am lucky to have them, but it's not the same. I don't think I could ever hate you, and I hate that you think that way. You are so stubborn, Amelia. It is infuriating!" Teddy was lightly rubbing her leg almost like a nervous twitch; he stopped at these words, staring at his hands clenched in a ball in his lap.

Amelia sighed, "Teddy, I had no idea, I'm so sorry. Well, I have to say you picked a terrible choice for a second attempt at love. I'm a crazy hot mess that can't even figure out happiness to save her life, and I have a ton of baggage. You are very lucky to have the support you do though, they love you very much. I know I'm stubborn and difficult to be around, I can't help it. I am doing the best I can, can't you see that?" She was straining her voice to be heard as it cracked under the pressure.

Teddy was irritated. "You can't help who you fall in love with, I had no idea love would be something we would talk about tonight, but everything about this relationship has been a complete surprise. I need to go clear my head. I'll take you to bed, and I wrote you a letter. You can read it after I've left." Amelia agreed, feeling that nothing she said could change his mind. He tucked her in with everything she needed. "Goodnight, Amelia," he said, but his voice was cold.

Amelia was kicking herself. How could she hurt a man like Teddy? Sitting herself up, she opened the letter.

Amelia,

Now that you know about my past, I hope that you will give me time to bounce back. Stephanie's wounds when she left me were so deep that I still haven't healed. I have found myself wanting to be with you more and more. I wanted to tell you myself before you heard it from anyone else. I just want to be honest. I know three years is a long time to hold on, but I'm doing my best. I hope you will understand and believe me when I tell you, I care for you very much. I've never been good with words, so I'll leave my deepest thoughts in the words of someone else.

Wine comes in at the mouth, and love comes in at the eye; that is all we shall know for truth before we grow old and die. I lift the glass to my mouth, and I look at you and sigh.

-W. B. Yeats

xoxo Teddy

Amelia cried herself to sleep, holding Tune and wishing Teddy would come back home. She wasn't surprised, she messed up again. Hoping Teddy would forgive her for her sins. Her love for him was real, but their pasts had them both afraid and damaged. Could they ever see eye to eye on things moving forward? Amelia thought about this till the pain medications set in, and she couldn't keep her eyes

open anymore.

Chapter 10

Teddy walked for hours, pacing the vines in the vineyard, sick to his stomach. He wrote that letter, he felt that something like that would happen, he thought he started to understand Amelia, maybe he was. Teddy eventually found himself at his father's door. He sat on the porch, not knowing what to do or say. His feelings so jumbled, pain in his eyes, and his heart broken. He loved Amelia, her passion, drive, and her love for Tune was one of the first things that made him fall for her. She said she loved him, why is this so hard? Why can't anything be easy for him? These thoughts were on what seemed like a constant loop in Teddy's head.

"Son, are you okay? What's wrong? Come inside, it is cold out here." Ted slowly opened the door to greet his son's back on his steps.

Teddy jumped. "Sorry dad, I know it is late." He got up and wiped his face, slowly turning to meet his dad's gaze.

"Oh, Teddy, come on, let's talk. I'll get the bourbon." He walked into the den to the liquor cabinet, removing two glasses and pouring a small shot in each.

Teddy thanked him as he reached out to accept the glass and sat down at the table. "I love her dad, and everything is so screwed up. I'm scared. I don't know what to do."

"So, she told you huh. Is this what this is about? Her past, is bothering you, or is this about Stephanie?" He looked at him with a stern stare.

Teddy was shocked, "What do you mean so she told me? How do you know?" He was pounding his fist on his leg in anger.

"Calm down, she technically told you first, you two were just too stubborn to have the conversation, and I happened to pop in at the barn looking for you the day I returned. Now answer my question, son," Ted said calmly.

"Both, I think. It isn't so much her past, it's how much she lets it define her, and how she makes up other people's mind about what they think. It's infuriating, and yes she is stubborn. Then I told her about Stephanie, and all she kept saying was how lucky I was to have a family. I felt totally disregarded." Teddy was talking too fast; it was like a bottle of champagne when the cork is finally removed.

Ted sat there and listened before he spoke. "Son, unfortunately, you both have had some rough times in life. She wants everything you have, and you want everything she has never given anyone, and feel unworthy of your affection. Your mother had to teach me to love myself, before I could fully love her. Pain, death, and torture are three things that consume a person when they experience what Amelia has. You have to be patient and just continue to be there. If in fact, this is what you want?"

"I love her dad, I want to try, but I'm scared of being abandoned again." Teddy sighed

"Abandonment is something the two of you have in common. Start there, heal, grow together, and see how your relationship evolves.

You have time, you don't need it all today." Ted explained quietly while patting his back gently.

Teddy put his hand up on his shoulder to touch his dad's, sobbing hard. "How can I let go of Stephanie? I feel like she's stolen everything from me, leaving me with a huge void. It's holding me back. I need closure. I need to feel like I can breathe again."

"There, there, now try and hear me on this. Teddy, sometimes we can't have what we need in life, life is an uphill battle, and sometimes we meet defeat and have to accept it. Stephanie is your failure, try and accept it, and keep climbing towards Amelia. It is all about the journey, it's not always about the end result. If you can't forgive Stephanie, it will only hold you back from continuing with Amelia. It's your choice." Ted walked towards his bedroom door.

"Thank you. I'll let myself out, get some rest dad. Thanks for the advice." Raising his glass to his dad, he took the last sip and then left.

As Teddy walked out, he felt the instant smack of cold air. The wind was strong, and Teddy knew a storm was brewing. He knew he needed to go home, and check on Tune and Sapphire. Sapphire hated storms and usually tried to flee in fear. He was worried, they couldn't afford to lose any crops either, and they relied heavily on their grapes to keep them afloat.

Teddy kicked the dirt as he walked back, swearing under his breath, "Shit." Why couldn't he catch a break? As it was, he had been trying to come up with a new white blend for months, and it wasn't going well either. The vineyard needed a new release to help rev up business for the winery.

He got back home, and sure enough, Sapphire was trying to get out as soon as Teddy opened the door. "It is okay girl, I'm here, come lay down with Tune." Tune was snuggled with Amelia. Teddy came over and saw the tissues and dried tears on her cheeks. Teddy felt terrible that he created these emotions; he never wanted to make her cry. It seemed that they both had similar events separately, their past left them with a lack of trust, and failure, he thought. He sat down next to her, lightly rubbing her back. Teddy decided to go check the fire before bed and tucked the covers in around her.

As Teddy went out to the living room, he began to think back to his relationship with Stephanie. They were college sweethearts, together for six years. They had met in a psychology class during Teddy's second year in his business degree program. Stephanie was a freshman in college, and this was her first day on campus at Butler University. Teddy was immediately drawn to her. She was tall with blonde hair, blue eyes, and was gorgeous. Her smile could light up a room and he always found himself having to stop from staring at her in class. Teddy finally got the courage to ask her out, and she said yes. After that, they became inseparable. He proposed right after graduation, and they planned a June wedding three years ago now, except she decided to never show up, never call him again, never give him a reason why, and embarrassed him in front of everyone they knew. Stephanie's father came to the vineyard a week later to apologize and return all the gifts and the ring. Teddy thought back to himself throwing the ring out into the vineyard on the far west of the property. *Hopefully, some lucky person found it,* he thought, gritting his teeth. Teddy could feel the anger building in him as he sat in front of the flames; he hated that after three years, it all still had a hold of him. The only thing Stephanie's dad gave him for closure was that she wanted to do it before it got this far, but after his mother died, she didn't know what to do. That didn't really help, but give him more anger. Hiding behind his mother's death, coward! He got up, added another log to the fire, and headed back to bed, trying to shake off the memories.

He got undressed, closed the bedroom door, and got into bed with Amelia and Tune. Begging Sapphire to come lay with them, she finally jumped up, nudging Tune with her snout until he moved over to make room for her.

Teddy laid in bed, staring at Amelia and petting the dogs. His mind was racing, but completely content in watching her sleep. She was so beautiful, their little family could be potentially sitting in front of him. *Tune and Sapphire seemed happy, why couldn't we be?* Tomorrow he would try to work through these feeling with her, he thought. He snuggled up as close as he could, their heads almost touching, and drifted off to sleep.

Hours later he woke up abruptly to Amelia saying, "Teddy, Teddy, please wake up!" and shaking his arm.

He jumped up immediately. "What's wrong, what's going on?" he panicked, looking around anxiously.

Amelia looked terrified. "Sapphire and Tune are freaking out, hiding under the bed, and the wind is terrible. It sounded like a tree just fell outside. What is happening?"

Teddy jumped up, grabbed his phone and looked at it. He had 16 missed calls, and with that, he heard banging on the door and went running out to the front of the house. Sophia, Ella, Ted, and Todd were all standing there, hurrying to come in.

"Tornado coming in, we need to get in the basement now. Hurry up and grab Amelia, there's no time. The warning hit 7 minutes ago; we are running out of time!" Ted stammered flying through the front door, grabbing supplies and rushing everyone to the basement.

Teddy stood there for a few seconds before Ella screamed, "Move it!"

He quickly snapped out of it and ran to the bedroom, grabbing Amelia and rushing out of the bedroom. "There's a tornado coming, we need to seek shelter in the basement. I'm so sorry; I should have paid more attention to the weather. It'll be okay, I'll keep you safe." He kissed her forehead, placing her next to Sophia and Ella.

Amelia was freaking out. "Tune, come on Tune, Teddy, you need to get him now!" panting, she grabbed her forehead with her hands and started to cry.

The girls tried to soothe her as Teddy ran back up to get Tune and Sapphire. Ted came down with candles, food, and some water for all of them. Teddy finally came down with Tune and carrying Sapphire, who was whimpering.

"I should have known something was up when I was walking dad home, and Sapphire was trying to escape. I'm losing my edge lately." Teddy said to his dad, putting Sapphire down next to Ella.

Tune ran up to Amelia and laid in between her legs, licking her hands, and she was squeezing him. Sapphire army-crawled over to get closer to Tune, trying to bury her head under Tune's head. Teddy finished helping his dad get everything as prepared as they could, then he sat down behind Amelia holding her.

"You are freezing, let me grab a blanket." As he got up, she grabbed his arm, "please don't leave me," she sobbed slightly.

Ella got up and grabbed a few blankets from across the room in a storage chest. They all sat together in a circle around Tune and Sapphire. Teddy covered the both of them up and rubbed her arms to help calm her down and warm her up. Amelia was shaking, and Teddy was thinking how this couldn't have happened at a worse time, with them fighting and him leaving her, then abruptly waking up to a potentially very dangerous natural disaster.

Teddy whispered in her ear, "I'm so sorry, it's going to be okay, and I won't leave you."

Amelia needed to hear this voice, and his breath hitting her ear and neck so softly sent shivers down her spine. She gently grabbed his hand and squeezed it to let him know she heard him and appreciated it.

About a minute later, power was out, the house started to shake, and they could hear windows rattling upstairs. Amelia turned and buried her head in Teddy's chest; he held her tight and was rubbing her head rocking her back and forth trying to calm her. Ella was also leaning into his arm, worried. He wrapped his arm around Ella and Amelia grabbed her from the other side. The three of them huddled together. Sophia let out a little scream, and Todd tried to calm her." You need to stay calm for the baby." Everyone looked up at them in surprise, and Todd winced immediately.

"Whoops, that wasn't supposed to come out yet, high anxiety situation, I'm sorry Sophia!" Todd said.

Sophia looked at him furiously, then smiled. "Remind me to kill you when we get out of this mess! Well guys, not the way I planned to tell you that you're going to be aunts, uncle, and Grandpa. We are having a baby!"

Ted started to weep. "That is the best news. Sophia, Todd, congratulations!" He crawled over to them to embrace them.

Ella shrieked, "OMG, auntie status! When do you find out the sex?"

Before they could answer, a huge crash happened above them, making them all shutter and scream. Amelia reached out for Tune, grabbing him and pulling him towards them. Sapphire was trying to find an exit and Teddy scooped her up, and the four of them huddled into a ball holding each other.

Amelia looked up at Teddy, "Just in case we die, I love you. I'm sorry!"

Sophia and Ella gasped in excitement, becoming giddy, grabbing each other's arms.

"I love you too Amelia. But it's pretty much over, and we are going to be okay." Smirking, he bent down to kiss her.

Amelia grabbed him so tight into an embrace that she didn't even realize that Ella and Sophia were cheering in the background.

Teddy released her and everyone started getting up. " Wait," Teddy said, "let us go check first. Ladies, wait and stay with Amelia and the dogs please." The men headed out.

Amelia looked at them. "That was the end of it?" She was shocked.

"When they hit, it's usually quick, hopefully, the damage isn't really bad. Didn't sound good though," Sophia said while hugging Ella.

"We are safe though, it's good, and we just learned so many exciting things!" Ella said, her voice high pitched as she started to say something to Sophia.

Todd came back down. "It's not great news guys, because we got hit hard. A tree fell through Teddy's bedroom. He wants the dogs to stay down here, he is scared Sapphire will run." he said walking towards them.

Amelia gasped. "We were just sleeping there, we could have died if Sapphire and Tune didn't wake me up!" she said shaking her head and rubbing her arm.

"Another thing, Sophia, the car is smashed, high winds picked up it looks like. I'm going to have to go home and see what damage we have." Todd sighed as he walked over to her to hug her.

Sophia gazed over at him with tears in her eyes. "I don't care, at least we are all together and okay. We can replace and fix anything else."

Teddy came down to Amelia, rushing to scoop her up and twirl her around. "So you love me huh?" he asked, excited as he placed her back down.

"Yes, I want this, I'm scared. But I think you're worth it. I think we owe it to ourselves to try. Don't you think so?" She grabbed Teddy's face and pulled him towards her to kiss him passionately. She didn't care at the moment that everyone was watching.

To her surprise, Sophia and Ella were tearing up. After she let go of Teddy, they came over to hug her and to express how happy they were for them.

Ella was jumping the gun in excitement. "Yes, I'm hearing wedding bells!"

Everyone laughed at her and Todd said, "I think this deserves a celebration at the vineyard! Wine anyone?"

The next thing they knew they heard a huge thump upstairs.

"DAD!" Teddy screamed as he ran upstairs.

Chapter 11

Teddy came up the stairs and turned the corner to see his dad unconscious on the floor of the kitchen, not responding and not breathing. He yelled down for Todd, "Carry up Amelia NOW! Hurry! It's dad!"

Todd arrived and placed Amelia down next to Ted. Todd and Amelia immediately assessed his condition and started CPR. Amelia told Teddy to call 911.

For three minutes Teddy sat there and watched them work on his father. Finally, Amelia said, "His breathing is there but it's shallow, he's in cardiac arrest. Todd, we need to hurry!"

Paramedics arrived and quickly took over. Amelia sat back, trying to catch her breath. She looked up at Teddy. "Bring me to your sisters so I can update them. They must be so worried." Teddy said nothing, picked her up and brought her down to them and left.

The girls started asking her a million questions, both crying. Amelia held her hand to her chest and took a deep breath trying to gain her composure. "We won't know until the hospital runs some tests, but I think he went into cardiac arrest. Todd and I were able to get him breathing again, right before the ambulance took him. It is a good sign. We aren't out of the woods yet though." She sighed looking at them, wiping her tears away from her own face. "He's strong. He can fight this."

Ella and Sophia sobbed as they embraced each other. "Let's get Amelia upstairs and we can head over to the hospital", Ella said.

"No, you guys go," Amelia insisted. Someone has to stay with Tune and Sapphire. I think leaving me here is good, I don't want to risk Sapphire getting out. I won't be able to chase her."

"Are you sure, Amelia?" the girls asked in unison.

Amelia nodded as she held Tune. Ella and Sophia looked back one more time and thanked her before dashing off to the hospital.

Amelia took this time to check Sapphire out, her behavior was peculiar to her. It generally isn't normal to hide when their owners are there to comfort them. *Something is up* she thought to herself. She called Sapphire and Tune over and started doing an exam. Her nipples and glands were swollen and come to think of it, she had been less active lately. Amelia smiled down at her. "Sapphire, you pregnant little girl?" She rubbing the dog's head and caressed her as she waited. Soon, they could get X-rays and order her some prenatal vitamins to keep her healthy and strong.

Teddy and Todd followed the ambulance to the hospital. Teddy couldn't help but think that he met Amelia in a similar way. *That's hopefully a good sign, he has to be okay.* Amelia and Todd had saved his life. Teddy shook his head in the passenger seat, thinking how he couldn't lose another parent. Miranda, his mother, had left them four years ago now. Doctors said it was an aneurysm, but Teddy never was able to fully accept it. It was so quick, no goodbyes, another person in his life, that he felt he never got closure with in the end.

They had to wait in the waiting area for a while before the doctor came back to explain they needed to rush into emergency surgery if they had any chance of saving his life. "Yes, whatever you need to do to save my dad," Teddy said.

The doctor grabbed his shoulder. "Stay strong, my nurse will escort you to the surgery waiting room, where I'll come to meet you later. I just want you to know, it will be a couple of hours."

With that he whipped around and all Teddy could see what his lab coat like a cape flapping in the wind behind him.

Teddy was like a zombie following the nurse, replaying the last 24 hours on a repetitive loop. Shaking his head and his hands balled in a fist, till Todd reached over. "Teddy, your hands are stalk white, release your grip. Talk to me."

Teddy looked up. "Sorry, I didn't even realize, I can't believe this man. He has to be okay, thank God for you and Amelia with the CPR."

"I just hope it was enough, the stress from the tornado just set him off, then I stupidly got him more excited with the pregnancy thing." Todd brushed his hands through his hair.

Teddy reached over. "Don't you dare take that away from yourself. This is not your fault. It was probably the stress I caused, being over there around midnight complaining about Stephanie and Amelia. I drove him crazy."

Todd looked up, surprised. "Teddy, why didn't you tell me Steph was still bothering you? I had no idea, I could have helped you. That whole situation was messy, and it's her loss anyways.

"Thanks, but I just can't get her dad's last words out of my head. I feel like I have no trust in the dating department now and had no closure with her. Now, I feel like he was hiding that he wasn't feeling well, because he didn't want to bother us. The problem is that I never want to talk about my feelings, not that I didn't want to talk to you." Teddy said, feeling confused.

Todd sighed. "We will get through this."

Their conversation was cut short by Ella and Sophia rushing in franticly, looking for updates. Teddy and Todd filled them in, and they all sat down, exhausted emotionally and mentally. They were waiting for the doctor that they knew wouldn't be out for hours.

Teddy asked, "Where is Amelia?"

The girls looked at each other. "She told us to leave her, so we did. She said that someone should stay with the dogs. We asked if she was sure and she waved us off."

"She is probably right, but she can't even let them out or anything by herself. I should go back to her." Teddy said panicking.

"Teddy, you can't leave yet. Wait with us, we just got here." Sophia said anxiously.

Teddy got up. "You have Todd. I need to be home right now. I will come back. Let me get the dogs settled, and I'll come back with Amelia. I'll bring the dogs to dads', so I don't have to worry about the gaping hole in my house and them getting out."

With that, he walked out, so final and determined that Ella and Sophia were rendered speechless and watched him walk away.

Teddy got in his truck and drove home in a fog. Replaying everything that was overwhelming him with emotion. By the time he got to Amelia, he was in tears. He walked into the house and down to the basement quietly sobbing, as tears ran down his face. Amelia took one look at him and tried to get up to reach him.

"Oh, Teddy, no. No, he can't be gone. Come here!" she cried as she tried to reach him.

He stopped dead in his tracks and looked at her, shocked. "I'm sorry, no he's still in surgery. As far as I know, he's still alive," he said, bending down in front of her.

She reached up to him, her eyes glistening, and kissed him fiercely, running her hands across his chin and up his neck. Their bodies were intertwined, as if they were one. With their emotions on overdrive; they found themselves passionately tangled, naked on the floor, as if they were the only two people in the world. Their hearts pounding, blood rushing through their veins, they forgot for a while, of the turmoil that had happened just hours before.

After a while, Amelia sat up, and asked, "Why were you so upset when you got here? Talk to me." She was staring at him pensively.

Teddy looked away, almost as if he was ashamed. "I was just thinking about the closure I never got with my mom, Stephanie, and now possibly my dad. It constantly plays on a loop, and it got the best of me. I was worried about you. You've been through so much in the last month. Your cast should come off next week, therapy, and where we stand. I don't want to lose you too."

"One day at a time is all we can promise each other right now. Life is unpredictable and unfair sometimes. I've recently learned that it is all in how we react and respond to things outside our control that matters. Right now, I know I love you, and you love me. Let that be enough for now," Amelia said as she gazed into his eyes.

Teddy reached for her hand and gave it a squeeze, and Amelia took that as an agreement between the two of them. Tune and Sapphire were sleeping, cuddled in the corner. They seemed so happy with one another, and that made Amelia smile.

"Teddy, can you bring me upstairs to the bathroom? I want to change so we can head to the hospital," Amelia said as she took a deep breath

Teddy agreed. "While you do that, I'm going to bring the dogs to my dad's house, as long as there is no damage. We don't have to worry about them while we are gone."

About an hour later, they were in the truck and headed to the hospital when Teddy's phone rang. Ella's name scrolled across it and they looked at each other. Amelia held her breath, both bracing for the bad news. Teddy picked up the phone anxiously and Amelia grabbed his hand and waited. Suddenly Teddy was rendered speechless, as if caught in a flashback.

Amelia grabbed the phone, "Ella, what is it? He's in shock, I think!" she cried, staring back at Teddy.

Chapter 12

Teddy could barely hear Amelia talking to Ella as his mind warped into a flashback.

Teddy and Stephanie were out on a picnic in the vineyard, at their favorite spot. They had just packed up and got in the truck when his phone rang. Teddy remembered looking at Steph and rolling his eyes. "It's Ella again!" Steph looked over and gently slapped his arm. "Pick it up, it could be important!" all the while giving him the side eye. Teddy answered but all he could hear was loud noises that wasn't easy to make out. He caught a few words here and there. "Mom. Gone. Dead. Home." Teddy looked at Steph with a stone cold face, losing color as he listened. "Ella, slow down. Did I hear you right, what did you say about mom?" Teddy said quickly. "Teddy, mom's gone, dad needs us. Come home now." Ella screamed back, through her sobbing.

Teddy dropped the phone, Steph was holding his hand, horrified. Both looking at each other in shock.

"Teddy, hello! Come back to me." Amelia screamed while gently shaking his arm. Teddy snapped back to reality. "What, sorry. What did Ella say?"

Amelia looked concerned, "Are you okay? I mean, I know you're not okay, but what else is going on?"

"Can we talk about this after? What did Ella say?" Teddy said quietly as if he didn't really want to know. The uncertainty in his voice made it shake.

Amelia looked at Teddy with sadness in her eyes. "Ella said he's out of surgery, but they lost him twice and brought him back. He's in a medically induced coma. We can see him, but it isn't good news. They don't know if he will be able to come off the respirator; he isn't breathing on his own right now. I'm so sorry," she said as she reached to hold his hand.

Teddy lost it. He broke down, crying, and punched the steering wheel. Then he got out of the truck and slammed the door, kicking the dirt, and took off. Amelia slid over to the driver's seat and took off after him with the truck. She finally reached up and rolled the window down.

"Teddy, please get in, let's go to the hospital. Please, your family needs to stick together and be strong," Amelia pleaded.

Teddy finally stopped and dropped to his knees with his head in his hands. Sobbing, swearing, and lost. Amelia put the truck in park and tried to hop out. The pain was excruciating as she slipped out of the truck on to her leg. She didn't care, all she wanted to do is rush over to him. She barely made it to him when she collapsed, embracing him, begging for his touch. All she wanted to do was console him. Teddy put his head in her chest and completely melted.

She sat there rocking him. "Shhh, it's okay. I'm here. We will get through this together."

Amelia's leg hurt so badly that she was seeing stars as the pain it shot up her leg into her hip. She tried to hold back the tears, but a little whimper came out. That was all it took for Teddy to realize what she had done.

She didn't care, all she wanted was for him to feel better. She had never cared for anyone so much in her life, besides her mother.

Teddy tried to argue, but she just pushed back. "You're always worrying about me, let me worry about you for now."

He stopped arguing but repositioned her leg to make the weight come off of it. For that, Amelia was grateful. The relief was much needed.

Teddy looked up at her with gratitude. "Thank you. You shouldn't have done that. How is your leg?"

"It's okay. I don't care about that. I'll be fine. Let's go to the hospital. Your sisters are waiting!" Amelia said quietly.

He picked her up and placed her in the passenger seat, and they left for the hospital. They sat in silence for most of the ride.

"This is like when my mom died all over again. I can't take it. I feel like I'm having a deja vu. I don't want you to stay with me if you don't want to, no matter what happens next. Promise me, you'll be honest with me!" Teddy pleaded.

Amelia nodded, holding back her tears. She needed to be strong for him. She reached over and rubbed the back of his neck and ran her fingers through his hair to comfort him. He slightly moaned and moved his head back into her hands, showing how much he appreciated it.

Once they got to the hospital, he dropped Amelia off at the entrance in her wheelchair. She waited for him to come back and they headed up. Ella had texted the room number. He was on the cardiac unit, floor 7, room 57b. When they came in, both his sisters rushed over. Their faces blotchy, swollen, and looking upset.

Teddy hugged them and went over to see his dad, tubes coming out from everywhere. He looked dead; there was no color on his face. It was so weird to see him lying there, not moving or talking. The ventilator breathing for him, machines beeping; it was all too much for Teddy to handle. He backed away and stood outside the door. Sophie went rushing after him. Amelia thought she should stay and give them a moment. She wheeled over to Ted, grabbed his hand and started talking to him.

"Ted, we love you, we need you to come back to us, please! I know how strong you are, Miranda would want you to fight. Come back to us!" Amelia whispered to him.

With tears running down her cheeks, Ella came up behind her and hugged her. They both just stayed there in that moment. Praying for a miracle.

The doctor came in, and everyone turned to talk to with him. "My name is Dr. Jennifer Krandle, I'm the head cardiothoracic surgeon. I'm sorry we are meeting in these circumstances. I want to be completely transparent with you, this can go one of two ways. Your father could come out of this and need therapy to gain back what he's lost as far as strength is concerned or he could never regain the ability to breathe on his own and will be in a coma until he is no longer with us. I know this is hard to hear, but the next 48 hours will give us a better idea of what we are dealing with here. His heart stopped three times, once at home and twice on the operating table. He is a fighter, but I want to be clear with you all on what we are up against."

They all thanked her. She recommended that they let him rest and she would see them tomorrow for her morning rounds. She left, and they all just stared at each other, before Todd finally spoke.

"I think we should all head home, eat and get some rest. We will have to be back here early tomorrow, and there isn't anything we can do for him now," Todd said as he embraced Sophia.

Todd, Sophia, and Ella said their goodbyes and left first. Teddy said he was going to stay for a few minutes and they would meet them at Sophia and Todd's for dinner soon.

Amelia returned to Ted, holding his hand and stroking the top of it with her other hand. Teddy stood behind her, rubbing her shoulders. They sat in silence for a while, Amelia felt overcome with emotion.

Amelia asked, "Can I have a minute with him alone? If you don't mind Teddy?"

Teddy kissed the top of her head and walked out. Amelia looked back with tears in her eyes to see if he was out of the room.

Amelia whispered, "I've asked my mom Kathleen, to watch over you, to send you back to us. I've never shared this with anyone, but I wanted to read you the last words my mom ever wrote to me. I hope it helps give you the strength to fight for your life, for us. We need you, Teddy and the girls need you. Your grand-baby needs you." She said as she took his hand in hers.

Amelia took a deep breath, wondering if she would be able to say her mom's final words to someone else. She was shaking, but something was telling her it was time. Ted needed these words. After all he's done for her, how could she not give him a fighting chance?

"Amelia, my sweet, the life you have lived, is not the life that I wanted you to have.

Be brave my sweet, for sweet and innocent was something that was taken from you.

Life can be so unfair, so fickle, remember the strength you have.

Be strong my sweet, for I can no longer be there to have you lean on me.

Death is not scary, it is not lonely, I will always remember what we had.

Don't follow me, run away from this dark place that we have been in.

Be loving my sweet, don't let anyone take that from you.

Your battles, take those scars, and learn from them, don't let them mold you.

Life can be amazing, find it, and don't let it go.

Be open to love, let it consume you, and enjoy the ride.

Just because my life didn't end up that way, doesn't mean yours shouldn't.

Be the light in the darkness, Be the guidance for someone in need.

Love, be kind, be humble, be smart, and remember your promise to me.

Remember my favorite saying and use it when it comes in handy.

Let me live on through you, I will always be in your heart, as long as you're open to my love.

As always remember, I'm a whisper away, the reflection in your mirror, the beat of your heart."

I'll always love you, and you will someday realize what this all really means. When you find that person, that family. Share my words to help guide someone else to peace, my love. Take this last gift, let it heal you, love you and embrace the journey ahead.

Love from Mom <3

Amelia, sobbing, put her phone away. The world spinning around her. She grabbed his hand and fierce fully said, "Fight! Mom, please help him." She squeezed his hand on his bed. As she did this, she felt his body move, jolting slightly. She lifted her head to see him gagging and his eyes open wide, gripping Amelia's hand. She immediately hit the call button, but it didn't matter, sensors were going off like crazy. Teddy came dashing back in the room.

"What is happening? What did you do?" He asked, looking menacingly at her.

Amelia stammered, "He's awake, trying to breathe on his own."

The nurses came running in, pushing them both out of the way and outside to wait.

Amelia looked up at Teddy as they leaned against the wall. "I have something to tell you." She beckoned to him.

"What? What else is wrong?" Teddy said exhausted.

Amelia smiled at him. "Sapphire is pregnant. Looks like 4-5 puppies. Won't be sure till I can take an x-ray."

Shocked, Teddy said, "Tune isn't fixed?"

"Nope! Kept saying I was going to do it, but school kept getting in the way." Amelia said exhausted.

At that moment, they heard loud noises coming from Ted's room. Amelia grabbed Teddy's arm and squeezed it, praying everything would be okay. Teddy and Amelia exchanged looks as they waited patiently for someone to update them.

Part 2

3 months later

Chapter 13

Amelia walked into the newly renovated house, the sun shining through the windows, her left leg finally allowing her to be independent. Amelia couldn't help but take full advantage of her new found freedom now that she could walk! Loving the breeze and that autumn, her favorite season, was around the corner. The renovations were finely done, and she couldn't help but feel overwhelmed with emotion. Teddy was very interested on Amelia's opinions and tastes when it came to redecorating the bedroom after the tree fell through it in June. The space that they created was theirs as a couple and it made Amelia beam with excitement. She never felt like this before, towards anyone, in her life. Teddy and Amelia were doing well, with small hiccups along the way that she blamed mostly on the stress of her injury, the house needing to be repaired after the tornado, and the vineyards financial state. But all that was to change, if Kathleen and Ted's children had any say about it. They were going to fight till there was nothing left, none of them could imagine losing the farm. One of the go big or go home moments for the winery was happening today!

Pevotella's Vineyard was hosting their first wedding. With Ted being in rehab, Teddy, Ella, and Sophia had an opportunity to have a few smaller events to show Ted just what they were capable of. The summer events had a great impact on the vineyard, but they were far from being in the clear, financially. Ted was coming home tomorrow and things were finally getting back to normal. Amelia was so grateful for the Pevotella family, and Teddy for taking her in to his life. The family for being there for her during one of her most difficult times and making her feel so included; between planning Sophia's baby shower, to listening to her opinions when it came to the vineyard and of course giving her so much hype as the "new" vet in town.

The wedding was all they could concentrate on today, though. Sophia would be there any minute to pick her up, so they could finish decorating, and Ella was busy setting up the stage for her band to play tonight. Ella had already called Amelia five times today to talk her off the ledge of canceling the band for tonight's gig, her nerves were getting the best of her. Amelia encouragingly explained to Ella how amazing she was and how the band would have never asked her to sing with them if they didn't think so. Amelia reminisced about how Ella got in a band and how much her life had changed in the last month and half.

It had been the vineyards first karaoke and food truck event, and it was a hit. After a while Ella decided to get up there and sing with her friends and have fun, to encourage more people to sing. The crowd went wild and everyone including Sophia and Teddy were shocked at just how well Ella could sing. That very next day, a local band called "Ladies in Blue," came to the vineyard and asked Ella to be their lead singer. Ella had always loved to sing, and decided to take a leap and try it out.

Tonight was their first gig as a band, their debut, and the lead guitarist was the one who recommended the bride and groom to have their wedding at Pevotella Vineyards. Ella told Amelia this night could be their big break, and a great way to get into the wedding industry for next year, if this all went well. Two other couples were coming tonight to see how their weddings are done, and if they liked it, the vineyard would be in a great position. On top of her new gig, Ella also baked their wedding cake. She always baked goods for the winery to sell with their wine, but never a big cake like this. If all went well, this could be great for the vineyard and Ella!

Teddy had been out with Todd since early this morning, doing god knows what. They both had been so secretive lately that it was putting Sophia and Amelia on edge. The both of them didn't needing any more stress. Sophia was seven months pregnant now and her belly was huge. Amelia had her last day of therapy last Friday, and had finally started to feel like she had her body back. Everyone had been stressing over Ted, his health, and if he would regain his strength from his heart attack.

All of this had created a beautiful friendship for Amelia. She felt like she had a best friend again and gained two sisters. She suddenly found herself unable to imagine a life without them. This scared her, what if it didn't work out? This sometimes limited her, she would find herself recoiling in effort to protect herself, but as always

Sophia would sense this and push it out of her mind. Amelia would call it her motherly instincts already kicking in, and Sophia would just wave her off. They found each other so embedded in each other's lives that Ted and Todd would joke who was with who. This would make them giggle and Amelia felt her fondness grow more and more for someone she never thought she would be friends with. She learned from Teddy that, in the past, Sophia had been rude, short, and uninviting to girls, especially Stephanie. Teddy and Sophia got in a bad way after the breakup because Teddy blamed her for driving Stephanie away. He eventually came around to realizing it wasn't her, but Amelia knew how easy it was to place blame elsewhere. Sophia did admit that she was very protective and closed off on purpose and how her instincts have been pretty spot on. Amelia told her that there is nothing wrong with limiting your circle, you're an amazing person, and honestly, it's better to have a few reliable friends then a bunch of flakes.

Finally Teddy rushed in, talking fast about how the dogs weren't eating like usual and his concern for them. "It's those damn snakes, upsetting them. Sapphire seems so restless!"

Amelia brushed him off about the snakes and said, "Nonsense, but I will check on them later, I'm sure they are fine. Sapphire isn't due yet, she still has a few more days."

The dogs had been acting up lately, though Amelia and Teddy have been cautiously optimistic about the new puppies Sapphire was about to have. She knew Sapphire would be nesting over the next few days, but Tune and Sapphire were out roaming the vineyard with Rhoda this morning, to give them some exercise before the big night. Sapphire wasn't eatinglike usual, so Amelia knew it was getting closer to the big day and was hoping she ordered everything she'd need to give her a healthy and easy delivery.

With so much going on, they were grateful for Rhoda, and all her help with the farm and the animals. Rhoda loved animals and reptiles and has been helping Amelia with her snake, Esmeralda, and her 10 snakelets. They hatched over the summer and had been a handful. Three eggs never hatched, for whatever reason, so they only ended up with 10.

Amelia had become the towns go-to, always someone calling or stopping by asking her questions and for her to examine their animals. Amelia and Rhoda delivered a foul and two calves over the summer. Teddy has been pushing Amelia to open a clinic at the farm, but with her physical state, she had been putting him off about it. Now that Amelia was doing so much better, they had been seriously talking about turning the barn into a shelter for animals she was caring for and to build a veterinarian office next to it. They had the land, and the nearest vet was 45 minutes away. Todd and Teddy were to start construction on the building, as soon as the permit and supplies were delivered. This excited her. She would be able to have a reptile, farm animals, and dogs and cats in her clinic to care for. Her dream of owning her own clinic was becoming more real every passing day. Between the new clinic and making wine, she had been so out of her element and extremely busy, but all she could do was smile about it. Amelia wouldn't change a thing.

Teddy had spent the summer working on a new blend for the vineyard and was getting close. Amelia was so interested in wine making, that she started dabbling herself. It was a nice way for them to spend time together, and Amelia was not able to be on her feet the whole time, that it was a great way for her to sit and fiddle why he ran around checking acidic levels, and tweaking temperatures. They had a bet on whose would be better. Amelia had already named her wine, but refused to share because she didn't want to jinx it. The new wine was set to debut in a few weeks at their next food truck/ music Saturday. They had been heavily promoting it, hoping this would create buzz and produce a good crowd for them.

However, making wine wasn't always fun and sometimes created stress on Teddy and Amelia. Todd and the girls were constantly asking how it was going, if the labels had been ordered yet, what it was, and if they could try it. This only made them more anxious and this caused them to bicker a lot lately. Amelia was constantly thinking how bad this could go, if neither wine was drinkable. Something they worked so hard to build up could end up being their biggest down fall. The vineyard needed this to work desperately. Ted took a lot of convincing as well, what if all the grapes they used went to waste because these new blends weren't good? They weren't in a favorable spot and Amelia knew this made Ted worry. He was so tired, from surgery and going through rehab, that he just couldn't put in the energy to argue and just told them to be careful. He said it was time for him to step back a little and it was good thing too, because he just couldn't do it all right now. He confided in Ted that, the fact of the matter was, he couldn't do anything at all and he was losing control, and admitted that this made him feel vulnerable and depressed. He had lost Margaret two years ago and now he was at risk for losing the vineyard. Margaret's sweat and blood went into making this vineyard thrive; Ted told his son that he couldn't lose his last connection to her. He begged Sophia and Ella to be extremely careful with the money they were spending, it was their last reserve.

With Amelia finally able to contribute to things on the farm, she found herself enjoying the land and outside more and more. Some of her vet supplies were trickling in, she was elated with how things were coming together. There is always work to do, they had run behind with everything going on. The energy couldn't be better, she thought to herself as she walked the vines.

Chapter 14

It was 11:30pm and the wedding was over. They were exhausted. The barn that they held the wedding in had been transformed with a beautiful, modern country theme full of canary yellow, lavender, and ivory. The place had been heavily used tonight and you could tell by looking at it. The general response from everyone seemed very positive, and the Pevotella family was feeling optimistic. Amelia was walking around cleaning up the tables, wheeling around a hamper for the linens and a garbage can. Teddy came up behind her, put his arms around her waist and his chin on her shoulder, whispering in her ear. Amelia melted. She had longed for his touch all day. She instantly sat back into his chest and Teddy swayed back and forth. He swung her around and Ella started to sing *Forever*

Love by Reba McEntire for them, beaming down at them as Teddy led them across the barn floor. Amelia smiled so big at Teddy that it hurt her cheeks. *What a beautiful ending to the day* she thought as she slow danced. Teddy sent her out for a spin and when she turned back around Teddy was on one knee.

"Forever Love, I promise you, I won't give up on you, no matter what." Teddy tried to sing to her. "Amelia Kathleen Pawsky, will you marry me?" he asked, holding out a beautiful vintage ring to Amelia.

Amelia couldn't believe it. She gushed at him while completely in shock. "Teddy, oh Teddy, Yes. Yes!" She rushed to him to kiss him.

Teddy beamed, picked her up, and twirled her around. "I love you so much, Amelia!"

"I love you too, Teddy!" Amelia had tears in her eyes and her voice shook nervously.

Ella, Sophia, and Todd came running over to them to congratulate them and to celebrate. Suddenly, no one was tired anymore.

Sophia and Amelia were talking. "That's my mothers' wedding ring. Dad gave it to Teddy a few weeks ago to size up for you. We are so happy to have you in the family."

Amelia sobbed silently. "I can't believe this, and I don't know how I got so lucky. I don't deserve you guys!" She hugged Sophia, swaying back and forth.

They stayed up celebrating until the clock suddenly said 2am. Teddy said, "We really need to get home to the dogs. See you tomorrow everyone. Ella thank you. Your voice is really something," as he bent down to hug Ella.

They all waved goodbye and were off to bed. They had an early morning tomorrow too. They had to be at the rehab facility to pick up Ted at 9 in the morning. Amelia couldn't wait to tell Ted all about her proposal and thank him for the ring. It was so special to her, she thought as she rubbed her finger across the bottom of the band.

Teddy and Amelia walked in to find Tune excited to great them. "Where's Sapphire buddy?" Teddy said as they closed the door.

He called for her, but nothing. Then Amelia said, "Lets follow Tune, he'll bring us to her."

Sure enough she was in the basement hiding. Teddy started going off about how he was right to have worried earlier, urging Amelia to examine her, and figure out if it was time.

"Teddy, can you bring her upstairs, please, so I can have proper light to check her out." Amelia beckoned.

Teddy did as she asked and the four of them went into the living room.

Amelia stammered in shock, "I have to check to make sure, but I think she's going into labor Teddy!"

"No way, you said she had a few more days. Surely it isn't time yet. I'm not ready!" Teddy stared wide-eyed at her. "Can't be? Can it?" he asked, looking more and more surprised by the second.

Amelia did her examination. She was most certain that she was going to go into labor any time now. She checked her temperature, and sure enough her temperature was lower than usual. "It all makes sense, this is why she was hiding downstairs. Usually dogs find a safe place that is hidden to have their pups, it's their way of protecting them." Amelia said without looking up. "I wouldn't be surprised if she has her litter of pups by the morning."

Teddy looked pale. "We aren't ready for children, what are we going to do? Tune what did you do!?" he cried, looking over to him.

Amelia giggled. "This is exciting, I've only delivered one litter in school, but it is fascinating. Looks like I'll be pulling an all-nighter. They will be fabulous parents, you'll see," she said as Tune licked Sapphire's ear.

"What do we do? What's next? Is she okay, she looks so sick!" Teddy was now pacing back and forth across the living room.

"If you can help me make up a nice bed for her out here, and I'll need my vet bag and some pads, so we don't ruin the blankets." Amelia said softly.

Before she could even turn to look at him, he was off to the barn to get the supplies. Amelia texted Rhoda to see if she was up, and she thankfully was. Within a half an hour she was over to help her for the long night ahead. Rhoda has been a godsend to Amelia with her veterinary work. She honestly didn't know what she would have done all summer without her. She knew that it wasn't every day that you find someone who likes animals and reptiles and doesn't mind getting their hands dirty.

Rhoda came with coffee and an update on the snakelets. She named them all after wine. Amelia was amused and wished her luck telling them apart at this stage. Rhoda waved her off. "They're Chardonnay, Merlot, Riesling, Chianti, Cabernet, Pinot, Noir, Rose, Blanc, and Grigio." She beamed as she said this to Amelia.

"That's awesome, we will have to separate them soon. We can put an ad out to see if anyone is interested in buying one. We shouldn't keep 11 of them. We can keep few, but that's all. Agreed?" Amelia said gently.

Rhoda bowed her head. "I've gotten so attached, and wondering, may I have one to keep here? Noir is my favorite and we can keep Esmeralda?" she asked, almost in a begging tone.

Amelia thought this was a great comprise and agreed. Teddy came back with everything and they set up her bed in a big cardboard box. Sapphire was definitely straining and whimpering in pain. All Amelia could do was coach her through and talk to her soothingly. Teddy was making Amelia go crazy and beckoned him to sit and be helpful or to go the bed room with Tune.

"Sorry, Sorry! Fine, we will go then. Please take care of her and if you need me yell!" Teddy said, panicking as he kissed her forehead and rubbed Sapphires head.

Within the hour, Sapphire was pushing out a watery discharge and Amelia was relieved. "Good girl Sapphire, almost over, keep pushing girl!"

About 7am, Sapphire was cleaning her puppies. Amelia was right, five beautiful puppies were born. She and Rhoda got some wet cloths, cleaned up Sapphire and helped her clean her puppies, and the area as best as they could before sitting back. Exhausted but wide awake, they sat there in awe of how beautiful life was, having just witnessed one of life's beautiful gifts.

"Looks like I have some naming to do," Amelia said to Rhoda as she got up to get Teddy and Papa Tune. "You little rascal" she said to Tune as she bent down to tell him the good news. "Teddy, Tune should stay separate from Sapphire and the puppies for a while. Sapphire might become very protective of her babies if Tune approaches. We have to be careful," she said to Teddy before opening the door. "We will have to keep him on a leash and distance them. We need to see how she responds."

Teddy looked shocked. "But they love each other. Sapphire would never, no. Really?"

"Yes, we need to be careful!" Amelia urged.

Teddy did what she said and left Tune behind for now. He wanted to go see his baby. Teddy approached by her head and talked to her first to give her warning he was there. She looked up and wagged her tail slightly.

"You can pet her now, she is okay with you being there. Believe me, we would know if she wasn't." Amelia said smiling.

"So much blood, Amelia. Is she okay?" he said nervously.

Amelia promised it was normal and she was fine. She was thrilled all five were nursing. Amelia would need to order a scale to monitor their weight. It would be a long month ahead for them now. There was one that looked just like Sapphire, a chocolate, a black, a tan and one that was white. Quite the array, but Amelia wasn't surprised. Tune had black nose and darker skin tone, so she knew there was possibility of darker pups!

Amelia thanked Rhoda and told her to get some rest. She called Sophia and Ella, beckoned them over immediately, without telling them anything. In hindsight she shouldn't of, because they were worried, but she wanted to surprise them in person.

They melted instantly. Amelia was very protective, so she took them to see Sapphire one at a time, to make sure she was comfortable later that morning. Sapphire was such a good dog. Amelia explained how that wasn't the case usually. She hasn't growled or seemed bothered at all yet. She was hoping it would stay that way. Tune was so upset to be kept from her. Teddy brought him out on a leash, and kept him in the kitchen where he could still see, but far enough away to be safe. Sapphire noticed him immediately, but wasn't wagging her tail. Amelia pointed this out to Teddy. "She isn't ready for any male dog to be near her puppies. We need to respect that boundary. She will let us know when she's ready," she explained to Teddy.

Teddy told her to sleep on the couch while he and Ella went to get Ted. "Sophia and Rhoda are a call away if you need anything and we will be back later." He kissed her before walking out the front door.

Amelia was exhausted. At this rate, it didn't look like they'd be giving any puppies away. Rhoda, Todd, and Ella had all expressed that they would like a puppy. She recalled Ella saying how she thought one would be good for Ted too. Teddy told her from the beginning they were keeping one. So that was five already spoken for. Amelia too exhausted to debate and continued to monitor Sapphire to make sure she was doing well.

Once everyone left, with Sophia thankfully taking Tune with her, she laid down on the coach and passed out. It wasn't till Teddy got home hours later that she woke to him softly kissing her cheek.

Amelia sat up. "How's Ted doing? How'd everything go today?"

"Dad's fine, I think all the exciting news, exhausted him. But he is doing well. Do you want to go see him quick?" Teddy asked, sitting back, clearly exhausted.

Amelia walked over to Ted's to visit for a little bit and stretch her legs. It had been an emotional rollercoaster the last 12 hours between the proposal and the arrival of the puppies. She was elated that it was all good news for once, and now Ted was home and things could truly go back to normal. She knocked on the door and then entered Ted's house.

"Hi Ted, it's Amelia, I came to just say hello quick!" She cautiously walked into the kitchen.

Ted yelled from the other room. "In here, come on in! So sweet of you to pop over." He smiled up at her as she rounded the corner. "How are you my dear?" Ted said softly.

"I'm tired but wonderful! I'm so happy you're home and okay. I've missed you!" Amelia said lovingly.

Ted blushed. "You're too kind to an old man. I must tell you something, I've wanted to tell you for a while, but didn't know how to do it," he said in a serious tone. "I heard you that night, I felt things that were so unusual that I thought it was a dream. I heard you kind voice reading to me. You helped me return, to wake up. I'm forever grateful for you and those kind words you shared. Did you write that?"

"No, my mom wrote me that before she died, it was the last thing she wrote to me." Amelia said weeping.

They sat there talking about Kathleen, Ted's near death experience and how life works in mysterious ways. He went on to say that this was one of the unexplainable miracle moments people talk about. This is how they must feel afterwards. He reached over and patted his hands on her shoulder smiling.

Chapter 15

Three weeks had blown by in the blink of an eye. The puppies were all doing well, walking, playing, and Tune and Sapphire were simpatico again. Ted was home and doing well. Teddy's house became the place to be, since the birth of the puppies. Their engagement party was tonight and Amelia had named their puppy Vino. He was the white puppy in the litter and was perfect for them. Their family was growing, and they couldn't be happier. Todd and Teddy were done building the outside of the clinic and were diligently working on the inside. She had sent out flyers to announce their grand opening in 8 weeks.

The vineyard was holding its own, and the wine debut was tonight. Teddy figured that they should do both events together. That way they had something to celebrate regardless of the wine outcome. Amelia was getting ready when Teddy came in to the bedroom, shirtless with his blue jeans on. *Man did he look fine*, she thought to herself. At the moment, he was wiping his face in a towel, and looked up to find Amelia leaning up against the door frame with the handle of her makeup brush twirling in her teeth. She was wearing a sexy bra and underwear set with a lacy garter belt and black thigh high stockings. Her hair was pulled to one side.

He walked over to her and bent down to kiss her. "You look stunning," he said, running his hands down her waist. He picked up her and carried her to the bed. He laid her down and softy kissed her from her neck down to her belly button. Amelia moaned softly while running her hands through his hair. She sat up and twisted herself on top of him, thrusting him down onto the bed. He laughed in a surprised way and stared at her lovingly. Their romantic moment was exactly what they needed to set the mood for the evening.

They got ready, and Amelia loved it when Teddy got dressed up. He was so handsome and looked amazing. Amelia wore this ivory dress Sophia found while she was out shopping one day. It was knee length, one shoulder and had a shear overlay to top off the look. With beautiful wedge heels and a light shawl, she was ready. On the way over to the big barn, they talked about how nervous they were for the debut of the wine.

"What if they are both bad?" Teddy asked nervously

Amelia smiled and grabbed his hand. "Babe, what if they are both good?"

He smiled at her. "Love it when you're the optimistic one. You always have a way of calming me, it's one the things I love about you the most."

"Surprising, huh! And do tell me all the things you love about me!" She smiled sexily at him and squeezed his hand.

Ella and Todd were already there setting up. They walked in and were instantly blown away. It was beautiful. Burlap table cloths with white lace runners down the middle. There were clear turquoise mason jars filled with sunflowers, baby's breath, and greenery. The jars had twine tied around the top and a votive candles on each side. On the dessert table was a beautiful two tier white cake with burlap and lace, wrapped around the bottom layer and sunflowers flowing up the left side. Everything looked so perfect. The table had a beautiful sunflower arrangement in a burlap covered square vase, with twine holding it together at the top.

On the table to the left of this were two wines covered in burlap, waiting for the big reveal. This immediately made Amelia's palm sweat. She was so nervous, despite the front she put on for Teddy. What would Ted say if they were both bad, how embarrassing? She had to shake that feeling off, bad vibes were never good for her. She had to remain positive, she said out loud to herself as she paced back and forth.

Ted came over to her. "Amelia, dear, are you okay?" He stopped in front of her, holding a cane.

This was the only way he could get around good lately. Therapy was helping, but it was a struggle to regain his strength on the right side.

"Oh, yes, I am. Just a tad nervous. You know, it's a big day. Of course you know, sorry!" Amelia blushed and looked at her feet.

Ted placed his hand on her chin. "No matter what, today will be a beautiful day. We are celebrating you joining our family!" Staring into her eyes, he spoke softly. "I have a good feeling about these wines!" and turned on his heel to go talk to Teddy.

Ella came over to her and they talked through the evening plans. "Where's Sophia?" Amelia asked.

"Her ankles are so swollen from the pregnancy. She's exhausted, Todd's leaving to get her now," Ella said

Sophia wasn't due till December 6, but with her being 38 and already having issues, the doctors were worried about preeclampsia. Amelia and Ella both exchanged concerns about her making her safely to her due date, and of course didn't want her to miss her own baby shower in a couple weeks.

People soon started to fill the barn, about 100 people in total. The pressure was on. Ted was walking up to the mic to start the night. The evening was going amazingly, and everyone was eagerly awaiting the reveal of the wine. Teddy and Amelia had walked up to the microphone to announce their wines when something unexpected happened. Drew walked into the barn.

Amelia stood there, confused and dazed, then walked over to a chair and sat down. Holding her head, she wondered, *what the heck, how did he even find me? Why does he want to?* The stress sent her into a flash back to a couple months ago.

Teddy and Amelia were fighting about her reaching out to Drew to tell him what happened. "He might be looking for you, he should know where you are and if you're okay don't you think?" Teddy stammered at her.

"Umm, no I don't think. He has made it very clear that he doesn't want a relationship with me, why would I purposely put us both in an awkward situation. He doesn't care that I can't walk, might not ever again!" Amelia was half yelling, half crying as she sat in her wheelchair.

They had just got home from a pretty bad session. Colin, her therapist, told her if things didn't start progressing, he feared she wouldn't regain the ability to walk. It was a bad ride home and Amelia tried to get out of the car and walk into the house to push herself and prove

him wrong and she fell, scraped her face, arm and leg up pretty badly.

Amelia stood up. *I swear if Teddy called him, I'm going to kill*

him. How dare he? Drew was approaching her, pale faced, and looked

like he was going to faint.

"Amelia, hello." Drew said, looking down at his feet.

Amelia whispered, "How did you find me? What is going on?"

Drew took a deep breath as he lifted his head to meet her eyes,

"Can we go talk somewhere privately?"

Just then she heard Teddy at the mic calling for her. "Where is

my bride to be?"

Everyone was laughing and looking around for her. She looked

at Drew. "Please give me a few minutes," she said, walking towards

Teddy.

When she got up there she forced a smile and stood by Teddy's

side as he gave his speech and revealed his wine. It was a burgundy

wine and it was delicious. They passed around a tasting size pour and a piece of dark chocolate as Teddy spoke. "I named this wine after my fiancé, Amelia, it is called *Amore Amelia*."

Amelia and Teddy clinked their glasses together and he kissed her so softly on her lips. Amelia reached for the microphone and said, "Please enjoy this to cleanse your palate and I'll be back in five minutes to debut my wine."

She walked away smiling, and Teddy followed her. Grabbing her hand, he said, "Are you okay, babe? What's wrong?"

"Did you call Drew behind my back?" Amelia stammered at him, looking menacingly

Teddy looked confused, "God, no why would I do that to you?"

"Then who did, because he just walked in, seconds before you called me up there." She looked over at Drew standing by the wine bar and then back to Teddy.

"Amelia, I swear, I didn't have anything to do with this." Teddy looked stunned.

Amelia walked away, tapped Drew on the shoulder and ushered him outside. They sat at a table on the back deck away from the other guests. "This is the best I can do right now, if I knew you were coming, I could have planned better."

Drew looked over at her, puzzled."I received a letter from you, stating what happened and that you are living here and engaged."

"What? Well, I can tell you I didn't write it!" Anger rose in her.

"Well, who did then?" Drew said, exhausted. "Tell me I came out here for no reason?"

Amelia sighed. "I'm happy to see you, I just didn't think you wanted to ever be in my life or cared where I was."

Drew looked at his hands. "I admit, I haven't been the most understanding person. But I do certainly care about you. I just didn't know how to move past my anger and let go of it. Mom would've wanted this right?" His voice croaked on the last few words.

"Yes, mom asked me to fix this before she died, but I didn't want to do it by throwing that at you. I wanted you to want to be in my life, not to feel forced." Amelia sobbed. "I'll never forgive myself for that night."

Drew reached for her hand. "Amelia, I know you didn't do it on purpose. I know Chloe would be pissed at me for not talking to you for this long. I'm sorry. I want to try and work this out. To build a relationship with you."

"Really? I would love that. I don't even know where you live or if you're dating or married or what? I would love to have a brother." Amelia's voice cracked in and out. "I have to go back inside now. How long are you here for?"

Drew said, "I fly back out tomorrow. I came for your engagement, but work is a nightmare. I want to tell you something about Dad, Amelia." Drew's tone turned serious. "Dad was in prison, in Arizona. He got arrested a year ago for drug trafficking. An inmate stabbed him to death two weeks ago. He's gone."

"Wow, I can't say that I have much emotion about it at this moment. He's been so absent from my life. I don't even feel like I've had a father all these years. Now I don't, at least I know where he is. Thank you for telling me." Amelia said, staring out blankly.

They sat for a few minutes catching up on major details before it started to get buggy out. Amelia got up and they hugged and walked back inside. Teddy was waiting for her by the door. He grabbed her hand and walked her to the mic, staring at her all the while. Trying to read her face.

Amelia pulled herself together. "In front of you is a subtle Rose wine, it has a hint of apple and floral notes at the end and I made this wine in memory of my mother, Kathleen. It is called *Sundazed*. I hope you all love it as much as I loved her." The label had a sunflower on it with a breast cancer ribbon wrapped around the stem and a picture her mom on the back. Amelia raised her glass and said, "This is for you Mom! Love you!"

Everyone was either clapping or wiping their eyes. Teddy and Amelia hugged and then took a sip. Teddy looked at her. "This is delicious! I'm so proud of you, thank you for doing this for my family."

Amelia kissed him. "I'm glad it's good, because that would have been awkward. I love you, and I don't know how I'll ever repay you for what you've done for me." she whispered.

Ted walked up to them and hugged them both. "Well, well, two amazing wines, thank you Teddy and Amelia and congratulations. There are ballot boxes on each side of the room. Please place your votes and if you'd like to purchase either bottle tonight you may do so at the wine bar. There is a very limited quantity available tonight. We will be donating to the cancer center in memory of Kathleen and thank all of you for your support."

There was a reporter there, covering the event and they were asked to pose for a picture with Ted and their wine bottles. The three of them took a picture and answered some questions before. The reporter explained how it would be on the news and in the papers in the next few days.

As Teddy walked away, everyone was clapping and Ted reached for Amelia's hand. "Can I steal you for a minute?" Ted starred into her eyes and grabbed her hands. "I'm sorry if you feel I betrayed your trust, but I found Drew and wrote to him. I thought he should know and did it while I was in the rehab facility. No one knew about this."

Amelia said quietly, "I can't believe you did this. I wasn't happy to be ambushed, but I am thankful for the reunion. He wants to start over, he wants to be a family." Tears ran down Amelia's cheeks.

"You deserve to have him in your life. I hope you can forgive me in time. I find I'm quite meddlesome in my later life. I don't know why? You can't be mad at an old man forever? Hopefully." Ted kissed her cheek and walked away.

Amelia couldn't even be angry at him if she wanted she to. She walked over to Drew. "I'd like you to meet Teddy before you go." She looked at Drew nervously

"Yes, of course. I'd love to." Drew said

Amelia and Drew walked over to Teddy, Ella, Sophia and Todd. "Everyone, I'd like you to meet my brother, Drew!" Amelia looked at Drew. "Drew, this is Ella, Sophia, Todd, and Teddy. These are his sisters and brother in law."

Drew shook their hands and he and Teddy walked off to get a drink. The girls and Todd looked at her shocked. "I'll explain later. All I have to say is this is all your dad's doing." Amelia said to them. They all gasped.

"Wait till I get a hold of that man!" Sophia said as she stormed off with Todd close behind her.

"Oh boy!" Ella exclaimed "This is going to be good." She started to walk away and then turned back to Amelia. "Are you coming?"

"No, no I'm going to take a minute." she said, exasperated. "I'll catch up!"

Amelia sat down at the nearest empty seat, took off her shoes and held her necklace in her hands. Amelia whispered, "Momma, I hope you were looking down on us today. Drew and I are talking again." Tears ran down her face. "I love and miss you so much." She wiped her tears and composing herself. She found Drew and Teddy and joined them for she didn't want to miss any more time with him.

Teddy and Amelia cut their cake and danced to a special song that Ella sang for them with her band. Sophia and Ella got up to make a toast to Teddy and Amelia. Todd and Ted stood on the sidelines snapping pictures of the special moment. The toast was beautiful, so beautiful that Amelia couldn't stop crying. Teddy gave a thank you speech and Amelia just waved as she tried to control herself. The evening was perfect, she was reunited with her brother, her fiancés family was amazing, and she felt like a princess for the first time in her life. Teddy continued to walk around praising her and she eager to introduce his fiancé to his extended family and friends. Teddy truly loved her and made her feel as she always felt lately. Special and loved.

At the end of the evening, Amelia asked Sophia to be her matron of honor and Ella to be her maid of honor. Todd would be Teddy's best main. They sat and excitedly talked about the baby being in a ring bearer or flower girl pulled in a wagon by the dogs! The evening ended in so much love and laughter. Drew was amazing and stayed till the very end. Amelia thought he tried hard to engage in conversation and really get to know everyone. She had never pictured them meeting Drew, but this encounter would have far exceeded her

expectations if she had any.

Chapter 16

Drew left that morning to go back to Colorado where he lived with his husband Patrick. They were finalizing adoption paperwork for a little 3 month old African baby girl. He was very happy working as a consultant for a law firm out there. Drew promised he'd come back with Patrick soon.

Amelia cried as the cab driver drove away with Drew in the back seat. So many times she'd been in this moment, but never this happy. She finally had her brother back. They talked about Elliot, prison, and mom. Both were exhausted, they were up till 4am talking. Teddy finally called it quits around midnight, and went to bed with Tune. Drew was fond of the puppies and Vino and he became fast friends. He couldn't believe the story about Tune and how mom picked him out for her. "She was always so worried about you, I'm glad she found Tune for you. He's amazing, and you can tell you have a strong bond."

The words she always wanted to hear from Drew came true that weekend. Drew forgave her. He was proud of her and all she accomplished. Drew was also sorry, a word she never thought she would ever hear. To actually figure out who was more sorry, ended up in a fit of laughter after a few back and forth of , "No I'm sorry, No I'm sorry!" from Drew and Amelia. They started texting regularly as soon as he left, normally a few times a week.

As October came to end, Ella and Amelia were finalizing everything for Sophia's baby shower tomorrow. Sophia was basically on bed rest at this point. No one would let her do anything. She was getting aggravated. Amelia tried to talk her through this, as she knew this feeling all too well. "We will come get you to hang with us or we will come visit. In two short weeks, the puppies will be big enough to go home with everyone. You'll have that to keep you guys busy too."

"We decided to name her Pumpkin, to always remind us of this special time in our lives." Sophia exclaimed. "She will be a perfect big sister to our baby!" Tears ran down her face.

Pumpkin was the exact clone to Tune and she was a handful. Amelia gave Sophia a hug and calmed her down. "This is one of the most exciting times for you guys. Embrace it and all that comes with it," she suggested. At that moment, Amelia's phone rang.

"Hello?" Amelia said, not recognizing the number.

"May I speak to Amelia Pawsky please, this is Tuft University." a women,said on the other end of the phone.

Amelia's eyes got big. "This is her, how can I help you?"

The women explained how they have been hearing a lot of buzz concerning her name and all she had accomplished in Indiana and wanted her to give a speech and accept an award from the National Veterinarian Association November 16 in Massachusetts. Amelia couldn't believe it. She accepted the invitation and hung up the phone, completely stunned.

Ella asked her a ton of questions and congratulated her. "We all have to go, this is awesome. I've never been to the east coast before."

"You're not missing much in Massachusetts," Amelia chuckled. "I'd love for you to come, if you can get away for a few days. I never thought I'd be going back so soon." Amelia sat down, bemused. She called Drew and Teddy immediately to share the good news and they both said they were coming.

Amelia couldn't believe her good luck. She was astounded that they even found out what she had been up to here in Indiana. She'd been on cloud nine but was getting worried. The clinic was supposed to open in two weeks and she was getting paranoid that something bad was going to change her luck. Teddy kept reassuring her this was what life was like usually and her bad luck and sad times were behind her if she wanted to leave them there.

Sophia, Todd and Ted would stay behind because of the puppies and the vineyard. Not to mention, Sophia was not allowed to even work, never mind travel. Ella promised to FaceTime them, so they could see the moment and share in the celebrations. Ted exclaimed, "Looks like another party at the farm when you get back!"

Amelia barely restrained her laugh. Little did he know there definitely was—a surprise for his big 75th birthday now that he was doing better. The calendar was filling steadily, which was great for the vineyard. Two weddings coming up before Christmas and two already scheduled for the New Year. Pevotella Vineyard was finally on the map as a venue and Amelia and Ella had been working on his surprise since July. A very famous wedding magazine was coming to interview and do a photo shoot of Ted and his prized vineyard for his birthday party on November 30th.

Amelia and Teddy settled in for the night with a bottle of *Amelia Amore*. They sat in front of the fire with the dogs and talked and kissed and talked some more.

"I've missed you so much!" Teddy said whole heartedly

Amelia smiled. "I haven't gone anywhere, babe."

"We've been so busy, I feel like I haven't *seen* you seen you." He smiled in his mischievous way.

The next thing she knew, the two of them rolled around the living room, making love and "making up" for lost time as Teddy would say. Amelia loved him and couldn't imagine life without Teddy. They were always making plans and he was constantly thinking of her, doing sweet little things to let her know he loved her. Little notes and poems sprinkled in the weirdest places for her to stumble upon throughout her day. Just last week, Teddy left one under a rock by the clinic. "I hoped you would find it and it didn't become a message in a bottle situation," Teddy exclaimed.

"That's so sweet babe, but it was so windy, it almost blew out of my hands and also message in a bottle. More like message in a vine." Amelia said lovingly to him.

She leaned over to kiss him goodnight, gave Tune a few bedtime snuggles and off to sleep she went. Tomorrow was the baby shower and it was going to be busy.

Ella beeped at quarter to 9 to pick her up. Amelia rushed out after giving the puppies their food and shots. She couldn't believe how big there were already. Amelia thought about how she could seriously stare at them all day and be content. She loved being a veterinarian and a pet lover.

Amelia called Teddy in the car. "Can you feed Esmeralda before you go out today? It's feeding day and Rhoda and I are busy with the shower."

Teddy sighed. "Of course, not my favorite thing to do, but anything for you. But you owe me," Teddy said laughing as he hung up

Amelia shook her head as she put the phone away. "You ready for this! I hope she likes it."

Ella yawned. "She better. Do you know how hard it is to through a shower when you won't find out what you're having? I tell you, no consideration for us." They both burst out laughing

They talked about what they had to set up and the wine menu for the day. Ella had baked a beautiful red velvet cake with ivory colored frosting, and a mini burlap pendent banner that said *Baby* Shower. Peonies and greenery were delicately placed on a wood slice. The cake was two layers and looked stunning. The nursery theme was nature, so there were white birch accents and woodland creatures sprinkled about the barn. The tables were done with her favorite flowers, ivory and pale pink peonies with green hydrangeas. The table cloths were ivory linens with burlap runner; with wood slices under the clear, short round vases that held the floral arrangements. Pine cones, and ivory birds sprinkled throughout the tables with votive candles and lastly the gift table and five logs, one taller than the next with word B-A-B-Y spelt across in wooden letters, one on each log. The barn again was transformed into a beautiful venue that was hopefully just what the mommy to be wanted.

Sophia walked in, or wobbled in, at 11am and looked thoroughly delighted. She even cried a few tears. She looked beautiful in her long white dress that was long sleeved and V-necked. A floral belly belt tied around her to help show off her bump. Her hair was half up and half down and the red hair was really prominent today, Amelia noticed. Sophia was glowing and being pregnant really looked good on her. Though, it definitely wasn't good for her according to the doctors, she was having a hard time. She needed to stay quiet and relax so that she could carry the baby as close to full term as possible. The doctor already scheduled her a c- section on December 1, and she was on strict instructions to elevate her legs to keep the swelling down. Ella set her up and she was fussing.

"Surely, I can walk around a little, Ella!" Sophia said irritated.

"Oh, I'm sorry, do you want to into labor early? NO you don't Sophia. You will sit here with your feet up until your guests arrive." Ella starred her down as she walked away.

Sophia sat there and huffed loudly and watched as the two of them ran around last minute finishing up.

The shower was lovely and Sophia was exhausted after four hours. Todd came and picked her up, showering her with a beautiful bouquet and a kiss. He said hello to everyone, packed the car and off they went. Ted and Teddy came over and helped them clean up before heading home.

Amelia said, "Come on guys, lets go have dinner. We can finish tomorrow." She was exhausted as she plopped down in a chair.

"We are really getting good at this Amelia!" Ella sounded half surprised and half excited.

They shut the lights, locked up and headed back to Teddy's for dinner. Thankfully Teddy was an amazing cook. Otherwise, it would have been take out today. She laid with two puppies on the floor, enjoying the kisses and puppy snuggles. Minutes later, Amelia was snoring so loudly that Ella and Ted were cracking up.

"Man she is tired huh Teddy!" said Ted.

"You should hear her at night guys, this is nothing." They laughed harmlessly as Teddy walked over and covered her with a blanket, kissing her forehead.

Chapter 17

It was opening day at the clinic. Teddy and Todd set up burlap tape to run across the door and they had a little grand opening cutting ceremony. They all stood in front with her as she cut the tape and of course they celebrated with wine.

"Wishing you all the success in the world, my dear Amelia!" Ted said as he hugged and kissed her on the cheek. He whispered. "I'm rooting for you!"

Amelia couldn't believe that she had her own clinic that Ted allowed her to build on the vineyard land. As she walked through it for the first time today, her mouth was wide open in awe of how beautiful it all looked. The barn that Teddy and her spent so many moments in together, good and bad, was now transformed into a rescue farm. Stalls and pens set up for all she could need and more. Esmeralda and her remaining babies were moved into their own tanks. The puppies made their big debut today too. They ran around in a cute little pen set up in the barn. 'Not for sale' hung on it, because people wouldn't stop asking. They made appointments for people's pets and someone dropped off duck they found in the middle of the road.

"Aw, our first stray!" Amelia said "It's a female, let's call her Autumn. I can't believe she didn't get hit. I wonder where she came from." Amelia questioned the man who dropped him off and Teddy and Todd drove out there that day to make sure there wasn't any stranded.

Sure enough, Teddy came back with three more ducklings. "They were trapped in a ditch off the side of the road. Poor things." Teddy sighed as he handed them over. "How did you know Amelia?"

"Honestly didn't know if you would find eggs or ducklings, there should have been more, I hope they didn't get hit. Usually females are laying eggs or with their brood, which ranges from 7-12 ducklings." Amelia said "You could have found nothing too, I just wanted to make sure."

Teddy knew that voice. "I'll go check again," Teddy said as he was walking back to his truck.

Amelia smiled and thanked him with a kiss before he took off.

Amelia and Rhoda checked out the ducklings. The mother duck was so happy to have them back with her.

Rhoda said, "She still seems off? You think they missed some?"

"Either that or they died. Let us hope Teddy missed them the first time." Amelia said nervously.

Eventually, the day wound down and Teddy did return looking filthy. "Do you know how hard it is to chase a duckling?" He handed her a box with four more ducklings covered in mud.

"They must have got stuck and couldn't make it to the ditch. That's why Autumn was in the road, she was probably trying to get them." Amelia smiled brightly and thanked him.

Rhoda took the box and went to clean them up. Teddy gave Amelia a look that read, you owe me, then left to go get cleaned up.

Amelia excited discussed the hours and the schedule with Rhoda. Rhoda had talked to Ted and he agreed to allow her to work both the winery and the vet. Everything was going according to plan and Amelia needed to get ready for her trip to Massachusetts soon. Rhoda would manage calls and care for the animals staying there till Amelia was to return. That was still a week away and she hoped to be more settled before she had to leave the clinic already.

Over the next week, the "Wags to Whimpers" clinic sign was hung and a rescue farm sign as well. It was creating a lot of buzz for the vineyard. People would come to check out the farm and sample wine. It was a great thing for children to see and for the parents to taste some wine and desserts. Ella had started baking again now that they were busier. They all were working 24/7 chipping in and making this as successful as possible. For once in a long time, Ted didn't seem worried about losing the vineyard and it was amazing to see him walking and smiling again.

It was a big contrast to when Ted first went into the rehab clinic. Teddy had inadvertently found out about his dad's plans when a gentleman called to ask if he decided to sell or not. Teddy had been furious, Amelia recalled.

"No, we aren't selling. Thanks anyways." Teddy said as he slammed down the phone and stormed out to his truck with his dad's things. "I can't believe he didn't tell me. Wait until I get a hold of hi—"

"Don't you dare go at him like that Theodore!" Amelia yelled. "He is hurting and trying to get better. You either have a calm conversation about it or nothing at all. Do you understand me?"

Teddy starred wildly back at her, then melted back. "I understand, but I can't believe him. I don't understand." he said sheepishly.

"You can yell and scream about it all you want to me, but he can't handle that right now." Amelia hugged him. "I know you're frustrated, we will figure this out. I promise"

Amelia smiled. *And so we did* she thought to herself as she tucked the ducklings safely in for the night. *We made a great team and Teddy is a great man.*

Over the next week, Amelia found she was getting busy with clients and her rescue farm was getting fuller. Since her grand openings, she now had two malnourished and injured geese, one with a broken leg and one had a broken wing. She would mend their injuries and she and Teddy discussed letting them live around the pond on the property.

"There's a little sprinkler fountain in the middle and there's fish and muck in it. They should like it there." Teddy said

Amelia smiled. "That would be perfect and they will make their own nesting area to sleep once they acclimate to the area in the spring time. For the winter we will have to keep them in here till they are fuller back to health," Amelia explained.

They had 8 ducks and the geese and ducks should get along well, she thought. They could live in the pond too. Amelia knew they could all survive in the cold, but with the pond not being treated and it needing cleaned up, she wanted to wait till they could do that for them. She didn't want them getting sick.

A couple of families had dropped off hamsters, guinea pigs, and rabbits, with notes on the top that just said "Sorry" or "Thanks," or the one she hated the most "kids grew out of them." Amelia would rather have them then they live terrible lives that were neglected. With the cold approaching, they had taken in a tabby cat that was always waiting for her to open the barn door. Teddy built it a perch on a window inside for her to sleep on. After that she never left.

Teddy joked, "Um, so we own a cat now."

"Yes, thanks to your kind heartedness. Reba loves the perch!" Amelia replied with a big smile.

"Reba, huh! I like it!" Teddy kissed her as he swept out the barn, rubbing Reba's head before leaving. She purred away looking after him before going back to sleep.

Tonight they had to pack to leave in the morning. They had a 6am flight. Ella, Teddy, and Amelia would be meeting Drew in Massachusetts in the morning. Amelia couldn't wait to see Drew and to visit her mother's grave, but she was nervous. She practiced her speech on the animals and tried to practice introducing herself to people and getting use to saying Dr. Pawsky. She wasn't use to this type of attention and she almost couldn't wait for it to be over. She liked her life here and was eager to get back, even before they left.

Teddy and Ella couldn't wait to get there and were being so supportive. Amelia tried to explain how life in Massachusetts was different because of her accident and time spent in juvie. They told her to try to enjoy and embrace the moment. They wouldn't have asked her to come if they didn't want her to. Amelia thought they were right, but still nerves controlled her most of the morning. She couldn't sleep on the plane and didn't feel any better when they landed either.

Just a day here, that's all Amelia. You can do this, she thought to herself. She paced back and forth at the hotel waiting for Drew to arrive. They were all going to get breakfast and head to the grave site after before taking them sightseeing for the afternoon. She couldn't shake this weird feeling something bad was about to happen. As much as she tried to put it out of her mind, it was like someone or thing was trying to warn her to be careful. This made Amelia anxious and regret coming more and more by the minute.

Chapter 18

Amelia met Drew in the lobby of the hotel and they set off to the gravesite. She asked Ella and Teddy if they would mind giving them this time alone to bond again. They happily obliged and said they would go out sightseeing till they returned. Teddy kissed her goodbye and off they went.

Drew and Amelia were like to chatty cathys the whole way to the grave. They stopped to pick up two sunflowers and then walked the rest of the way, as it was right down the road. It was so strange to be back.

"I never liked living here," Drew confided. "Mom and now you are the only reason I would ever come back. I miss her, now that I'm older, I wish that I didn't miss so much time with the two of you.

Patrick tells me all the time that it's never too late to start over. He can't wait to meet you!

Amelia listened patiently, nodding occasionally and smiling at Drew. "I'm glad Ted reached out to you. I just never thought you wanted to hear from me again. It's been really lonely for me since the accident. I lost everyone but mom. She was the only person who would talk to me. Even when I was with Elliot, I still felt lonely. Now I know why, he wasn't right for me and he was mean". Amelia smiled. "Patrick seems amazing, I can't wait to meet him too! I'm so happy you found your person Drew."

As they entered the grave site, they both became quiet. Amelia led the way to their mothers grave and immediately started to clean around it. When she was finally finished, she stepped back and looked over at Drew.

"I usually keep it so neat, but with me being gone, it really has overgrown." Amelia shuffled her feet nervously.

Drew took a deep breath. "Thank you for doing that. It honestly looks better than the others here. I know she appreciates it." He put his arm around her to pull Amelia in for a hug.

After a while, they both got up and placed their sunflowers on the top. Amelia touched the grave and said, "Momma, I'll be back again soon." before turning on her heels and walking away to give Drew some privacy.

As she started to look around, trying to not stare, she noticed a man in a baseball cap that seemed to be trying to hide from her. This made her put her guard up. *Who is this person* she thought, *is he spying on me or am I paranoid being back here*? She decided to wait and watch him before saying something to Drew. She didn't want to make him upset either. It was probably nothing she kept saying to herself.

Drew came over to her quickly and she was thankful to get moving. Every few minutes she would look behind her and Drew finally asked her what was going on. Amelia tried to act like nothing was wrong, but he didn't buy it.

"I know it has been some time, but you always were a terrible liar. So just save us both the time and energy and tell me what's going on!" Drew said sternly.

Amelia sighed. "It's probably nothing, but I've had a weird feeling all day. And I just saw a man at the grave hiding near a tree and it looked him he was spying on us. This town always puts me on edge. Don't worry about it!" As she turned around to look over her shoulder, she said, "Okay, never mind, he's following us right now. Do not look, I don't want to tip him off that we know, if he hasn't already figured it out." Amelia said anxiously.

Drew and Amelia picked up their pace to head back to the hotel. As soon as they walked in, they went straight to the elevators. They walked right past Teddy and Ella, Drew staring at the doors of the hotel waiting to see if he'd come in. When the elevator opened Amelia and Drew got in and Ella and Teddy rushing over, worried and confused. Just as the elevator door closed Amelia saw the man walk in, looking for them.

Teddy hugged Amelia. "What is going on guys? Drew, why is she so upset?"

"There is someone following us or Amelia. She saw him at the grave and then he followed us here," Drew explained. "That's why we went straight to the elevators, hoping to get on before he could get to us. Sure enough, he walked in as the door was closing. I don't think he saw us though."

Immediately, the four of them went to the hotel room, locked the door and sat down trying to figure this out. It didn't make any sense, who would be stalking her, who knew she was home? Ella starting googling and there was an award gala flyer that highlighted her accomplishments, so it wasn't as quiet as she thought. *People did know she was coming, but who would care?* Amelia thought to herself.

"I don't know who would know that I would go visit my mom's grave and where it is? Or that I was here already?" Amelia questioned nervously. "Drew, did you tell anyone you were coming?"

Drew shook his head."No, just Patrick and my work."

This was scary. Teddy wanted to call the police, but Amelia refused. The cop would probably say it was too early to report, without anything happening or knowing who it was. Because of all this, they decided to stay in the rooms together for the rest of the day instead of going out. They would order room service and get ready together for the gala.

"I'll protect you, no one will hurt you." Teddy told Amelia

"I don't want anyone getting hurt because of me. I always cause trouble, this is why I'm better off alone. I can't hurt anyone anymore." Amelia sobbed.

If she was being quite honest, she was terrified. She knew life was too good to be true. They started getting ready and Ella tried so hard to take Amelia's mind off of this guy.

"Let me do your hair and makeup. We can get ready together and have some girl time," Ella said as cheerfully as possible.

Amelia smiled weakly and agreed. They were talking in circles at this point anyway about this mystery man. They got ready and ate some food. Ella and Amelia wore beautiful gowns. Ella had a long A-line dress on that was a beautiful emerald green color. Amelia wore a navy blue dress that had a v neck line and went straight to the floor, with rhinestones bedazzling the bodice. Drew and Teddy wore black and grey suits and looked very handsome.

As the moment got closer to head out, Amelia felt her anxiety heighten. At this point, she could care less about giving a speech. She was more worried about the fact that he would be waiting for her and what he wanted with her. Amelia would never forgive herself if anything happened to Teddy, Ella, and Drew. These thoughts put her so distant from the others, as she sat waiting for the inevitable. She had a terrible feeling about this evening, and was kicking herself for agreeing to do this in the first place.

Chapter 19

Teddy said, "Amelia, it's time to go, are you ready to head out?"

Amelia had been sitting there oblivious to everything around her, as though Teddy's voice was miles away. Ella and Drew walked over and started trying to get her to come around to them.

"Hey there, you okay? You with us?" Ella said nervously.

Amelia snapped out of it. "Sorry guys, I don't think we should go. You guys stay and I'll go."

This created an outburst from everyone. "You're not going anywhere alone!" "What has gotten into you?" "Amelia, it'll be okay."

"I don't want anyone getting hurt because of me. I don't even know what this person wants or will do. I just can't risk having anything happen to you." Amelia said, standing up.

She was trying to be confident, hoping this would get them to acknowledge what she was asking.

The three of them shook their heads, stunned at her. "Why are you being like this Amelia?" Teddy demanded.

Before anyone could stop her, Amelia was gone. She had run out of the hotel room, and was moving fast. Teddy followed, calling her name, trying to get her to stop. He got to the elevator just as it was closing in time to see Amelia say, "Goodbye Teddy."

As the elevator closed, she broke down crying. She didn't want to hurt anyone, didn't they understand? She felt terrible for doing that to all of them, but Teddy, it broke her heart. She loved him so much, her love for him would end up being his demise. Ted was right, she couldn't keep running from it, it always would catch up. She was determined to see what this person wanted and who it was. As the elevator opened, it was to Amelia's horror that she saw him, dragging Ella out the door.

All she could see was horror on her face, trying to get away, but she couldn't. At once Amelia recognized the man. Elliot had Ella at gun point.

Amelia ran towards them shouting. "Elliot, let her go! It's me you want, isn't it?"

Immediately, he turned around, shooting a single round into the ceiling. The whole lobby screamed and ducked. Elliot then pointed the gun at her. "Well, well, look who decided to stop hiding from me. Come over here or she dies!" As he shoved the gun into her temple, Ella let out a cry.

"Amelia, run no, don't come here. He wants to kill you!" Ella said, sobbing.

"Shut up you stupid girl!" Anger rose in his voice. "Am I killing her, or are you coming. Don't be responsible for another death dear." He smirked with a disgusting look on his face.

Amelia came rushing forward to Ella and he dragged them both out the door up to an unmarked car outside the hotel.

Amelia had never talked about her past with Elliot in detail. He knew she went to juvie, but she never told him what happen. He could have easily figured it out, but why does he care so much now. Trying to think fast about what to do, she looked back horrified as she heard Teddy and Drew's voices. The last thing she saw was them rushing towards her. They weren't fast enough. Elliot hit Amelia over the head and chucked her into the backseat.

Ella screamed, "Teddy help!" as Elliot threw Amelia into her.

He had barely got the door closed and sped off before Teddy ran down the road after them. Ella's face was plastered against the back window shield crying and banging her fists.

That's the last image Teddy saw. Fear and anger coursing through his whole body, he looked at Drew and screamed, "Who the hell is this guy?"

Drew stammered, "It's Elliot! We just talked all about him since we've been talking again. He was very abusive to her, I just didn't think she meant physically."

They both stared at each other, not knowing what to do and shocked all at the same time. At this point, complete strangers were walking up to them asking them what was going on and if they were okay.

Teddy called 911 and gave the description of the vehicle to the operator. "It's a black Chevy Cruz, no plate looked like a newer model. The guy is about 6ft, had a tan baseball cap on with dark jeans, and a long sleeve navy shirt. We think it is a man named Elliot Turner that my girlfriend use to date. He has a gun and attacked Amelia with it before speeding off. Please help."

Teddy hung up, and looked at Drew. "Do you have any idea where he might be taking them?"

"Maybe school or Amelia's old apartment. I haven't talked to her in years, so I'm at a loss here as to what she did with him and where they hung out. I'm so sorry." Drew said nervously. "We will find them, we have to find them."

"Do you know where her old apartment was?" Teddy asked eagerly.

Drew sighed. "No, I just know it was close to the grave where our mom's buried because she use to walk there all the time from her apartment."

And with that, the two raced off to haul a cab, and head in that direction. Amelia and Ella's life were in danger and Teddy had never felt so nauseous in his life.

Chapter 20

Amelia woke up to her head pounding and blood dripping down the back of her head. Disorientated, she tried to focus her eyes and not move much, in an effort to figure out where they were. They were outside, and Amelia knew instantly were she lay was in front of her was Chloe's grave. *"May you live on forever in our hearts"* was engraved on the tombstone, something Amelia would never forget. She tried to listen hard but it was so quiet. Where were Ella and Elliot? she wondered. She contemplated sitting up. Her hands and feet tied, she decided to roll over to the side of the grave and use it as a rough edge to try and break the rope. Straining to hear any noise, she was so frightened.

She tried to move as fast as she could, the stone ripping her skin because of how hastily she moved. Finally, her hands were free, she untied her ankle rope and went to find Ella. She couldn't believe this. He definitely found out about Chloe, but couldn't understand why he was doing this.

The car was empty. She ran as quietly as she could to an old crypt with the door slightly open and light peeking out into the darkness.

As Amelia got closer she could hear Ella crying, begging to be let go. "What do you want with us?"

Amelia could hear footsteps as if Elliot was pacing back and forth. She heard him muttering to himself about killing Amelia.

"Too bad you're useless to me now, you are quite pretty, and maybe I'll have fun with you before I kill you." Elliot caressed her face before slapping it. His evil laugh filled the crypt. "She left me, I came back to an empty apartment, no note, no nothing. No one leaves me till I'm finished with them. I didn't tell her she could move, I don't know who she thinks she is moving away and trying to be happy somewhere else. Then I see on the internet, all of your pictures and she's engaged. That just won't do." Elliot yelled, getting angrier. "She doesn't deserve happiness, I thought I snuffed all the light out of her when I left that day. I underestimated her, that was my fault. So I nominated her for the stupid award to get her back here and it worked. She'll never be with anyone else but me. Why do you guys like her anyway, she killed someone, you know? When she wakes up, she'll find you dead too. Then she can see how she can never be happy again without me."

Ella looked at him bewildered. "You are crazy!" she yelled. "She will never take you back. She made a mistake and she did her time. She deserves to be hap-"

As she went to finish her sentence he kicked her hard in the stomach. "Crazy, you want to see crazy?" he yelled, attacking her again. Amelia snuck in and tiptoed towards the wall. Then peering from behind it, she saw them. Ella was tied up and forced in a corner of the crypt, sobbing. She could see three other handguns in a duffle bag and a knife. Chills ran up her spine.

Just as she went to make her move, she heard Teddy yelling for her. Elliot turned around looking frantic and ran right towards her.

Amelia, trying to think quickly, stuck out her foot and tripped him. He flew forward onto the ground, swearing as he fell.

"Where do you think you're going?" He grabbed her ankle and forced her to the ground. "You stupid bitch, I'm going to kill you and your friends here," he snarled as he wiped the blood from his lip. He got on top of her and started punching her, hard anywhere he could reach.

Ella screamed, "No, No, stop it, let her go!"

Amelia, searing in pain, fell into a flashback from juvie.

It was her third week there, and a group of girls were corning at her in the showers. Holding shanks and throwing punches, beating Amelia and cutting her multiple times. A guard found her covered in blood unconscious an hour later. Cleaned her up and threw her back in her cell. The next day, Amelia tried to kill herself and she was put in the hospital and had to meet with a psychiatrist. She was in the hospital till she stabilized from her injuries and then went to solitary. This is when she met Gretchen, her savior and the only reason she is still here. She helped her deal with her decisions, let go of enough guilt to not be suicidal anymore and helped her heal mentally and physically

from her trauma. She pushed her to start speaking at schools and

sharing her message. Gretchen gave her ways to deal with her

traumas and harness her emotions in ways that could be useful instead

of detrimental.

She snapped out of her flashback to the sound of a gun being
fired. She saw Teddy laying on the ground bleeding from his abdomen.
Amelia screamed as Elliot held up the gun to shoot at Drew. Her
adrenaline kicked in and she was running at him. Elliot turned the gun
on her and shot at her, missing the first time and hitting her in the
shoulder the second time. Drew tackled him and Elliot's gun flew out
of his hands towards Ella's feet. They scrambled and Ella inched her
feet forward to pick it up and lift it to her hands that were tied together.

Ella raised the gun and shot Elliot in the back, just as Amelia
grabbed the gun from the duffle bag and shot him in his side. Amelia
ran to Ella and untied her as fast as she could.

Ella was saying, "He's still not moving, hurry, he's still down."
She was crying and shaking violently.

Amelia removed the ropes and Ella ran to Teddy and she ran to Drew.

"I'm fine, let us get Teddy out of here." Drew said frantically.

Drew and Ella hoisted him up and Amelia took up the rear, walking backwards and keeping the gun pointed at Elliot. He was still lying there motionless as she rounded the corner. As she emerged from the crypt, the police screamed "drop your weapon!" Amelia placed it on the ground and put her one arm up as she winced in pain trying to raise the other. The police came running towards her, kicking the weapon away.

"He's in there" she motioned behind her as pain pierced through her back, flying forward onto the ground.

Gun shots firing rapidly from behind her. The pain was so bad that she passed out thinking, *this is it. I'm dying*.

Chapter 21

Amelia found herself walking a sunflower field, feeling amazing, young, and vibrant with no care in the world. She looked around and saw endless flowers in every direction and then saw her mother walking towards her. Amelia ran towards her, confused and happy at the same time.

"Mom, I've missed you so much. I love you. Drew and I are talking again. I fulfilled all my promises to you," she said as she reached out to touch her.

Kathleen moved back. "You need to wake up and fight, honey. You promised me you'd be happy. You need to go back to Drew, to your life. I love you, I'm so proud of you."

Amelia could see her fading away in front of her. She tried to reach for her, but she was gone. Amelia woke with a startle, frantically breathing and yelling, "Mom, no stay with me." Amelia woke up from what she was now realizing was a dream and she started to cry.

"Shhh, Amelia, it's Drew. Calm down, try to calm down, you are in the hospital. Mom's not here. Open your eyes, Amelia!" Drew said as he ran to her bed side.

Drew held her hand and filled her in on what had been going on. Amelia had been in the hospital for 3 days. She had two gunshot wounds and two fractured ribs and her orbit was fractured. She had several cuts and bruises. Amelia continued to look around, trying to gain a sense for where she was when she saw an award with an envelope under it, sitting on the window.

"Ah, yes, the committee chair who called you came over after she heard your name on the news. She felt terrible and was very apologetic. The police questioned her too. I don't think she had anything to do with it, she seemed genuinely impressed by you." Drew said cautiously.

Amelia sighed. "That was nice I guess. I'll read it later."

"How are you feeling, Amelia?" Drew asked at abruptly.

Amelia said, as if she it just occurred to her, "I don't care about me, what happened to Teddy and Ella? You are okay?" Amelia was talking so fast and her eyes were wide with horror as recalled what happened.

Drew took a deep breathe. "Teddy and Ella are going to be okay. Ella is with Teddy. He is recovering from surgery. Thankfully the bullet missed all his vital organs, he lost a lot of blood though, Amelia. He had to get a transfusion to replace the blood he lost. He's been a real pain the ass to be honest. He's been so nervous about you," Drew said smiling as he tried to make a joke. Which he realized that it came out wrong and Amelia wasn't amused, he said "Sorry, sorry, was trying to lighten the situation."

"Ella is okay? He beat her up pretty bad." Amelia said nervously.

Drew sighed, "Mentally, I think it took a toll on her more, but she is okay. I promise."

Amelia burst out, "Elliot, is he dead?"

"That bastard certainly is, and thank god the police were there. Otherwise, who knows what would have happened. You aren't in trouble for shooting him, don't worry. We all gave our statements, it was in defense of your life. Our lives!" Drew said encouragingly

The doctors came in and did some basic tests to see how she was cognitively and then agreed that she could be wheeled down to see Teddy and Ella. Drew brought her down to his room, Ella was so relieved to see her.

"Oh, Amelia, thank god. We've been worried sick. I have to call Sophia and dad," she stammered as she got on the phone immediately.

Drew and Ella left the room to give Teddy and Amelia some privacy. Even injured, he looked so handsome lying in the hospital bed. Amelia got up and walked towards him, bending down to kiss him. Teddy kissed her back and gently hugged her. Running his hand along her cheek, smiling at her like she was the most beautiful thing.

Meanwhile, she was bruised and swollen. *I must look ridiculous*, she thought to herself.

"Amelia, I'm so sorry, I couldn't protect you. I don't know what I would have done if something more happened the other night" Teddy said with tears running down his cheeks. "I love you so much. I can't believe we made it out. If it weren't for Ella and you. I would be dead," he said, looking down at his hands.

Amelia said with her voice shaking, "I'm sorry, I put your family and you in danger for a stupid award. It was all a hoax that Elliot set up to get me to come home. I don't ever want to hurt you again. I love you more than you'll ever know, but do you see how my life is. I can't have you mixed up in this." Tears welled up in her eyes.

"Don't you see, we are better when we are together? When we are apart is when things go to shit. Please don't ever leave me like that again." Teddy said squeezing her hand and kissing it.

Ella and Drew came back about twenty minutes later. "Well, if we can handle anymore news, we have a baby girl in the family. The whole thing ended up putting Sophia in preterm labor by a little over two weeks. Thank goodness, everyone is healthy and okay!"

"Oh my, I feel awful, but that's amazing! Nothing like some good news and us not dead to cheer us all up!" joked Teddy.

Amelia and Ella stared him down. "Her name is Evelyn Virgina Pallock, she was born at 8:08am and weighing 6 pounds and 2 ounces. She's 20 inches and she's perfect!" Ella exclaimed grinning from ear to ear. "When can we get the heck out of this terrible state and go home?" Ella chuckled.

"The doctor told me I can be discharged in the morning, Teddy any news on your end?" Amelia questioned.

The doctors were able to discharge them both in the morning and they scheduled flights later that afternoon. Thankfully it was only a two hour flight, otherwise the doctor would have made him wait longer. As it was, he was told he had to get a checkup in two days back at home. They were all excited to get back to their life at the vineyard and Drew couldn't wait to get home to Patrick. Teddy and Amelia planned to go out to see them around the Christmas holiday. Drew and Amelia said their goodbyes.

"I'm so sorry Drew about this whole thing. I don't know how this happened. He was never this crazy when we were together." Amelia said sheepishly

Drew looked her in the eye. "The police told us he had been an issue in town over the last month for being belligerent and got evicted from his house. This wasn't your fault! Promise me, you'll let this go. Please?"

"Okay, yes, of course. I'm just so happy you're okay and we are family again." She hugged him goodbye. "I'll talk to you soon, okay?" She walked away giving one more wave before meeting back up with Teddy and Ella.

A couple more hours and she'd be back home with her animals and Teddy's family. She couldn't wait to see Sophia and Evelyn and Todd. She just missed everyone and everything about Indiana. As they all got settled on the plane, Amelia looked over at Ella.

"I told you the east coast sucks!" Amelia said.

All three of them burst out laughing. Between Ted, this incident and her accident, she was all set with hospitals for a very long time.

Chapter 22

Ted and Todd met them at the airport when they landed and Ted had never looked more relieved in his life. He hugged all of them and kissed them, tears in his eyes.

"I was worried sick. I'm so thankful you are all okay." Ted said shakily.

In the car, the boys caught us up on all the activity over the last few days. Ted explained how Sapphire and Tune were absolutely nuts, it was like they knew something happened. The puppies and animals were all taken care of by Rhoda and the schedule at the clinic was filling up nicely.

"I can't believe all the people your rescue farm and clinic has brought already in the short time it has been established. This is going to be amazing for the vineyard Amelia. Thank you," Ted said.

Amelia smiled. "You are too kind Ted, Thank you for having me and not disowning me after this mishap in Massachusetts. I feel like all I've done is ruin things since I crashed my car in your small town."

They all told her to stop it. They spent the rest of the ride to the hospital just catching up and asking all about Evelyn. She would be going home in a few days and was doing well. It was such a special moment for Teddy and Amelia as Sophia and Todd asked them to be Evelyn's Godparent's when they got there to see her. Amelia cried as soon as Evelyn was put in her arms.

Over the next week, it was busy with a new baby, Ted's surprise party, and magazine shot. The Pevotella's had to be on their game and they were struggling to make it work. The clinic was busy and Amelia was slower than usual from her injuries still healing. *Thank god for Rhoda*, Amelia thought. She really was amazing and always a few steps ahead of Amelia in terms of things needing to be done.

Tune and Sapphire was so happy to see Teddy and Amelia that they stuck to them like glue. Amelia missed Tune so much that she didn't mind, but he always had a way of accidentally bumping her in painful areas. Sapphire just whimpered and licked them to death. The four of us laid together in bed the night before the party just holding each other, happy to be together. Ted and Ella took the puppies to give them a break until they were all healed up. Ted had named his puppy Landot after the grape. Amelia bought them matching bow ties for the magazine shot tomorrow. They all hoped he would be excited and enjoy the experience and the party. After talking for a while, the finally went to sleep.

The next morning, Amelia headed over to the barn after Teddy convinced Ted to go to town with him. He was so hard to keep everything from because he was always everywhere. Ella was already there with Sophia and Evelyn setting things up. The theme for tonight was black and white with touches of copper. They took a bunch of photos and printed them in black and white and hung them on clothes line around the room. The tables had black table clothes with copper

lanterns and small white square vases filled with succulents. The plates

and silverware were all copper and white linen napkins to finish off the

tables. There were copper wire lights providing the perfect ambiance

and a two tiered white cake with black paint marks swept on opposite

sides. On top was a simple "70" made out of copper wiring.

The wine special tonight was *Tres Blanco* and a new fall

sangria with fresh apples and cinnamon sticks. Everything was coming

together perfectly. Before they knew it, people where filling the barn

and patiently awaiting the man of the hour. Ted and Teddy showed up

fashionably late. When Ted walked in he chuckled.

"I was beginning to think they forgot about me!" he joked,

smiling at the crowd. "Now please do excuse me, while I got freshen

up!

Amelia walked Ted out. "Here, I got Landot and you matching

bow ties for tonight. You'll both look dashing, now hurry up and get

ready!" Amelia said as she gently pushed him to go home.

About an hour later Ted walked in a gray dress pants, a black button down, and his copper bow tie. Landot was on his leash with his matching bowtie and collar. Both of them looking as dashing as ever. The photographer starting snapping pictures and making all kinds of excited noises.

"Why did you guys get a photographer? You didn't have to!" Ted said, looking surprised.

Sophia handed Ted a letter. "Dad, this wedding magazine is here to do a photo shoot and interview you about the winery! You're going to be on the cover of the magazine in the spring edition!" Sophia smiled.

Ted couldn't believe it as the photographer swept him away to do the shoot. He was beaming, and the photographer was delighted with the images he got. The family all went outside to talk a group picture with the dogs at the end. Ted kept thanking the kids and expressing how he could of never imagined this and how Miranda would be so happy to see her vineyard in a magazine.

Teddy grabbed Amelia's hand and motioned for her to follow. They walked in the vines till they reached Teddy's pickup truck. There was a basket, two glasses and wine set all on a blanket in the back of the pickup with a radio playing music softly. Amelia couldn't believe how romantic it was. She got emotional when she looked at Teddy.

"This is beautiful. I couldn't believe you set this up. How did you have time? Amelia asked.

"My dad thought this is what I needed him for. Worked out for me because, I really wanted to do this for you and it kept us busy!" Teddy chuckled. "I love you, Amelia!" as he bent down to kiss her.

Teddy helped her into the truck and they sat there and watched the sunset. He poured her a glass of *Sundazed* and they made a toast.

"May we always have each other to get through an obstacle, confide in one another, and love till the end." Teddy whispered to her.

Amelia smiled, "Always, Teddy" she whispered back.

They took a sip and then kissed under the perfect sunset. Enjoying their first time alone in a while, feeling better, and happier than ever. Entwined in their love for one another, Teddy and Amelia laid there wishing for the moment to never end, all while wondering what the future held for them. As far as Amelia was concerned, this was the perfect life for her and she wouldn't change it for world. For a man to look at you longingly, like you're the only one in the world, is one of the best feelings she had ever had.

The radio started to play their song, *Forever Love,* Teddy immediately got up and put his hand out.

"Dance with me?" he asked looking down at her.

Amelia grabbed his hand, smiling, as he twirled her around dancing in the bed of the truck. Amelia laid her head on his chest, listening to him hum and sing to her. The sound of his soothing voice, grounded her, was her voice of reason, and always lifting her spirts. Closing her eyes, enjoying the moment and the crisp night air, there was no better place to be. Teddy made her feel so safe and secure, she swore she could stay in his arms forever. She looked up at the stars.

Amelia whispered. "I'm happy mom!" Smiling up at her, she saw a shooting star. Amelia knew, her mother was watching.

Epilogue

About three months into planning their wedding, Amelia had an unexpected run-in while in town getting supplies for the farm. She was loving that winter was ending and spring was upon them. She was walking down the aisle shopping for soup recipe ingredients when she heard a women say, "Excuse me, are you Dr. Amelia Pawsky?"

Amelia spun around. "Why yes, I am. How can I help you?" she said, extending her hand to shake the woman's.

"Yes, I was wondering if we could talk. I have some animals that need regular tending to and was hoping you'd be willing to take them on as clients for your clinic. We are also looking to re-home some of them too." The women looked at her as if she was sizing her up.

The whole interaction made Amelia's hair on her neck stand up. She didn't quite know what to think of the women. She and Amelia stared at each other until Amelia finally said, "If you will take my card and call my office. My assistant would be happy to set up a time for us to come out and check on the animals. After my assessments, I can give you a rate to give them regular care and see if we can take the animals. What is your name?" Amelia said inquisitively.

The women paused, then introduced herself, "I'm Mrs. Levey, and thank you. I will be in touch," she said abruptly before dashing off in the opposite direction.

This interaction was on Amelia's mind for the rest of the day. When she got home for dinner with Teddy she told him about this interaction. While Teddy found it peculiar, he also didn't recognize the name. They talked back and forth about how maybe they just bought farm land. Or maybe recently moved her and was new to the area. Either way, Teddy thought the business was a good thing.

"Rhoda will be with you too, it should be fine. I think we are just paranoid after the whole Elliot encounter last year." Teddy said comfortingly to Amelia as he kissed her forehead and starting clearing the table from dinner. "Come let us take Sapphire, Tune, and Vino for a walk to see Ella. She is having dinner with her new boyfriend and I want to go spy on her a little. It'll be fun!" Teddy said deviously as he looked back at her.

Amelia rolled her eyes at this, "Teddy, you should leave her alone till she's ready."

They went for a lovely walk through the vineyard. It was brisk, but they were all bundled in their jackets and Amelia and Teddy had on scarfs and hats to help with the wind. Even in the winter the vineyard was breathe taking. Amelia couldn't wait for their next wedding event and for Ted's magazine debut in the April edition of *Inspired Weddings*, it was one of the most famous wedding magazines out there right now. As they walked along, Amelia and Teddy talked about family, the clinic, and new wine ideas for the upcoming year. Amelia couldn't imagine a more perfect life than the one she was currently living.

Drew had called Amelia to update her about the adoption process. Patrick and Drew would be getting married this year too and just got word they would be adopting a 3 month old baby girl from Africa. They would be able to go get her on February 6 and Amelia was delighted. She loved having Drew in her life and he and Teddy got along great. She couldn't wait to meet Patrick in person and to meet their new little girl. They had asked them both to be in their weddings and Amelia and Teddy asked the same of them in return. Family was so important to Teddy and Amelia was finally starting to feel like she was a part of one. Drew and Patrick asked Amelia and Teddy to come out to Colorado next month when they got home from Africa.

Amelia was really looking forward to this. She had never been out that far West, and she was hoping for a much better trip with Teddy then they experienced this fall. It was to the point where they were able to start joking about it, which was good. Because Amelia secretly was worried Teddy would leave her after that happened in Massachusetts.

Sophia and Todd were doing well as new parents to a baby girl and a puppy but Evelyn was behind in her development and this was causing stress on them at home. They were going for some testing next week and the whole family was worried. Evelyn was a beautiful little girl in every way, but wasn't progressing as well as she should by 3 months and the doctors want to be sure everything was okay. Amelia felt that Sophia was suffering from Postpartum Depression as well. She was trying to figure out a way to talk to her about it without causing any more stress. She just wanted to help her feel better and get back to her normal self.

With everything going on in the Pevotella Family and Wags to Whimpers, Amelia was ignoring her own symptoms. Over the last few weeks, she hadn't felt like herself. She kept saying that it was just her emotions from her upcoming period and her being run down with all the commotion. She couldn't focus on her own issues because she was too worried about everyone else and she didn't want to worry Teddy.

The next day, she had a full day of appointments and they had two people coming to adopt the last snakelet, Grigio, and one of the guinea pigs. Amelia had to go out to a farm to check on a cow and a goat that were both pregnant as well. It was a busy day, but with Rhoda, it was always fun and manageable.

On their way home from their last house call of the day, Amelia asked Rhoda to drive. "I'm exhausted and don't feel that well, would you mind, Rhoda?" Amelia begged of her.

Rhoda looked over at her worried. "Amelia, are you sure you are okay? What's going on?"

Amelia waved her off and told her not to worry, she had just been feeling off lately and it was probably a virus going around. When they got back to the clinic, Amelia got out of the car, and went to get her vet bag from the back when she started having immense pain in her abdomen and was going in and out of focus. She fell against the car to catch her balance and then collapsed. All she could hear before she got lost in a flashback was Rhoda's cries for help as she laid there clenching her stomach, feeling some of the worst pain in her life.

Her front windshield broken, a man reaching out and pulling her out of the car and dragging her to safety. She could faintly hear his footsteps as they left her, she left hurt, a sense of loneliness, and fear; was she dying. Tune was licking her face, she opened her eyes to see a pair of beautiful green eyes looking down at her as he sat next to her holding her hand. He was talking to her in a soft comforting voice,

"You're going to be okay, I have your dog and the ambulance will take

you to the hospital."

Amelia remembered soft humming, and the first feeling of being safe

in a long time, that it instantly calmed her.

"Thank you." She barely got out as Teddy stepped out the way for the

paramedics to take over."

To be continued…